Animal Rights and Pornography

Animal Rights and Pornography

J. Eric Miller

Soft Skull Press
71 Bond Street
Brooklyn, NY 11217

Animal Rights and Pornography

ISBN: 1-932360-33-6
©2004 by J. Eric Miller

Cover Design by David Janik
ShortLit Series Design by David Janik and Charles Orr

Published by Soft Skull Press • www.softskull.com
Distributed by Publishers Group West • www.pgw.com

Library of Congress Cataloging-in-Publication Data

Miller, J. Eric.
 Animal rights and pornography / by J. Eric Miller.
    p. cm.
ISBN 1-932360-33-6 (pbk.: alk. paper)
1. Animals—Treatment—Fiction. 2. Sex customs—Fiction.
3. Sex crimes—Fiction. I. Title.
PS3613.I537A84 2004
813'.6--dc22
                          2004003513

The author wishes to thank
Jodi Hass
Hania Jurdack
and
Jennifer Trudeau

FOOD CHAIN

In a large and ancient family farmhouse at the edge of civilization, the mother, caught in a routine of cleaning and cooking, has long since become distant from the father, and he begins to fuck the only daughter. Eventually, the oldest son notes this and, half out of a sense of hunger and half out of a sense of wanting to possess and protect the girl, he begins to fuck her too. Taking part in a kind of silent power struggle, the father begins to fuck the oldest son in his ass. They go around like that for some time.

Eventually, the daughter and the oldest son reach an age where they don't appeal to the father as they used to. Without any more daughters, the father begins to fuck the middle son, who is now eleven. After about a year of this, the middle son begins to fuck the youngest son, who is nine. Another year passes and after about a year of this the youngest son tries to fuck the middle son but finds out he isn't allowed. Instead, he goes into the barn and begins to fuck the littlest sow in her ass.

Beyond the fact that the mother won't satiate the father's hunger any longer, perhaps the father starts all this fucking because something similar happened to him when he was a child; or perhaps it happens because when he fell from the tractor ten years ago and was unconscious for half a day—he never went to see the doctor; it might also be that the father is this way because this is what naturally happens when one is isolated with only a few people. Maybe it is all these things mixed up. Maybe it is none of them.

Regardless of why things are the way they are, this continual fucking culminates this morning at the breakfast table. The middle son has reached that age when he doesn't interest the father so much anymore, and the father went to the youngest son's bedroom last night to find that the youngest son was not there. This morning, he asks why. The middle son, who, as we know, has been fucking the youngest son, is silent. However, the father is told by the oldest son, who sits close beside the daughter, that the youngest son has been sleeping in the barn with the sow and its just-born piglets. It seems he thinks the piglets are his and wants to protect them.

The father nods. The mother's mother, a silent, very old woman, also nods. The father sits looking over the array of food on the cracked and stained china that has served these people for three generations. After a moment, the father gets up. He is pretty certain his youngest son can't be father to the piglets, but he doesn't want to risk the monstrosity of it. He puts on his boots in the mud room, goes outside, jerks the hatchet out of the blood-darkened chicken-killing stump, and goes into the barn.

The family continues to eat. The daughter asks the mother to pass the scrambled eggs. As they make their way from hand to hand down the table, everybody stops to listen to the wails of the youngest son, begging *No, Daddy, please don't hurt them* . . . and then the high-pitched screams of the mama pig and then the even higher pitched screams of a few of the piglets. All the cries blend together at the sound of the hatchet sinking down through something somewhat solid and into wood and then being pulled free and coming down in the same way again and again. The eggs continue down the table.

From the corner of her lip, the old lady wipes a dab of dark syrup.

BROKEN HARDER

What do you got in the box? the stripper asks him.

A pigeon, he lies. It was hurt and I thought I could maybe help it.

In fact, it was not a pigeon, but a rat. When he found the rat, it was crawling along in the street next to the curb of the sidewalk in the neighborhood of sex shops and strip bars. Its back legs had been smashed somehow and it was dragging them behind it. One of its eyes appeared to have been burst and the hair around it was matted.

Come on, Brian had said. There's nothing you can do.

But he'd wanted to try something. In an alley dumpster, he found the box.

He didn't want to tell the dancer it was a rat. Pigeon sounds better than rat, he thought.

She looks at the box and says, How hurt is the pigeon?

Pretty badly, I think.

Maybe you should kill it, the dancer says. Step on its head. That's the kind thing to do. That's what they do to horses that get hurt, they kill them. I love horses.

I'm from Montana, he offers.

Down here for Christmas break?

Yeah, he says. I talked my buddy into coming. He's got a brother who's moved down around here.

Christ, why would you want to come to the city?

Missing something, I guess.

This place will break you hard. Aren't you in a good place already.

I guess it's a good place.

Montana. Lot of horses up there, I bet.

Yes. He is a college student and grew up in the college town and has never touched a horse.

Lots of horses, almost everywhere, he says.

She stares at the box. Across from them, in an identical booth, his friend Brian sits with another dancer. A waitress in a tight, short skirt stands before them.

He looks at the dancer. You seem a little nervous, she says.

I don't mean to, he answers.

But he knows he is nervous. He's been nervous about the trip since he proposed it to Brian, and Brian had asked, What you think you're going to find there?

The waitress is standing in front of them now. What would you like? She sets two red napkins down.

I'm fine, he says, remembering what Brian's brother, who has learned the tricks of the city, had told them about the price of drinks in San Francisco strip clubs.

I meant for the lady.

Yes, may I?

Yes, ma'am.

She pauses for a moment, then says, Champagne, please.

The waitress nods. On the stage a pale and pudgy girl moves to the music. He is afraid of the girl. He is afraid of the dancer beside him and of the waitress. He has been afraid since arriving in this city, afraid maybe since leaving Montana, though he doesn't know why. He glances at the dancer beside him, just a girl, really, with a tight body and a lot of makeup. She looks the way dancers do on the television.

You're nice, the dancer tells him. I mean that, really. You look like the country, like somebody who grew up with animals and trees and all.

It was kind of like that.

I got lucky picking you. I just started here and I haven't had many nice people. You know what I'm supposed to do?

No, ma'am.

Sit somebody down and order champagne. It's a trick. Then when she comes with the bottle she'll ask for a lot of money. Most people are so surprised they just pay for it. We apply the pressure and they pay. I wanted you to know ahead of time, to be prepared. She leans back and releases his forearm from her grip. She says, I think it's nice about the pigeon.

The box is actually empty. He kept it in case he decides to go back and get the rat. But for now, he's lost his nerve. He tells himself it would not survive the night, not to mention the return trip. He thinks of Amy, and the apartment they share in Montana. Not long before he'd left, she'd said, I love you. He had not said anything in return.

The waitress approaches with a bottle and a glass. Forty dollars.

I don't have that kind of money, he says. His hands are shaking and he feels sweat on his face. Just get a regular drink for her. That's all I can afford.

The waitress stares at him for long moment, sees he's not changing his mind, and leaves.

Sorry, he tells the dancer.

She squeezes his arm but she not look at him.

The girl with Brian gets up and walks toward the stage. He buries three fingers in his hair and leans his head to one side.

I got to go, he says. He digs ten dollars out of his wallet and puts it on the napkin. Whatever is left is for you, he tells the dancer.

Brian slams the flat of his hand into a parking meter. Fifty bucks, he says.

Yeah. He is looking down into the gutter, though this is several blocks from where they saw the rat. They got me too, he lies.

They are still in the area of sex shops: flashes of skin, of plastic, of rubber, of chain. Signs promise 24 Channels pornographic action. Girls stand outside of strip bars hollering at them, Hey, come over here, come in here.

This place is fucking depraved, Brian says. I'm going down to Little Italy to wait in the bar for Terry. I've had my stomach of it here.

All right. I'll go on by myself for a little while.

You're not going to find it.

I know. I just want to walk.

What are you doing? Is this what we come down here for, to walk around and look at this shit?

It's just different here.

It's bad. Christ. Are you looking to get laid or something?

No, he says. I just want to see what this all is like.

Shit, Brian says, I've seen enough. Enough. Hey, don't you miss Amy?

Yeah, I miss her.

Brian says, You're fixing to take off on her?

No.

I see you. I know what you think. If you aren't careful some day you will be all alone wandering around neighborhoods like this for kicks.

What are you mad at me for?

I'm not mad. I just wish we weren't here. I just wish I knew what the hell it is you want.

I don't know what I want.

Maybe you just need to be broken harder, Brian says, looking away. Then you'll know a good thing for what it is.

He pretends to be just walking by, but then he gets down on his hands and knees to look under cars. The rat is not there. He peers up and down the sidewalk. A cop approaches, staring straight ahead.

He clears his throat as the cop is passing. The cop does not turn. Then he musters it: Have you seen a rat?

The cop stares at him. He feels like the cop knows he has been in the strip club. He feels like the cop thinks even worse of him, that he has been in not only a strip club, but also that he has been in many of the little stores up and down the street.

He says, Here, I mean. On the sidewalk.

The cop shakes his head and keeps walking. After three steps, he stops and turns back. What do you want with a rat?

Nothing. He walks away, stopping at the edge of an alley. It is dark and as he starts into it, he realizes a man is sitting against the wall with his legs jutting out. He steps back. Something beyond the man is moving through the newspapers, and he is certain it is the rat.

The man says, Hey, you got something for me? A little money? It's New Year's, isn't it?

No, two days yet.

Well, Christmas then.

He takes a dollar from his wallet and hands it down to the man. The newspapers are still. He is afraid to step over the man and starts back out of the alley.

Happy New Year's, the man says.

It has begun to rain.

He has dialed his Montana number. Amy?

Hey. You made it?

San Francisco.

The air is cooling and the raindrops coming down harder.

You sound so far away. The trip was good?

Yeah.

Well, what are you guys doing?

Wandering around the city. What are you doing?

Nothing. There was a blizzard that came in last night. Reading magazines, watching TV. That plastic you put on the windows is keeping it warm, though.

Cars splash by, drowning out some of what she says. Two men walk past, speaking a foreign language. One laughs and pats the other on the back. A wind starts.

I miss you, she says. Christmas was nice.

Yeah, I thought so, too. He looks at the skyline, buildings poking up against glowing gray clouds. He says, I almost bought you a pet rat.

She is silent. Then she says, I'm afraid of rats. Maybe I never told you that.

I guess I knew that. Most everybody is. What about pigeons?

Hey, I'm burning that candle you gave me, the one that smells like cinnamon and pine? It's nice. And it's burning really slow, so that even though I lit it an hour ago almost none of it's gone.

I'm glad you like it.

Wow, is it snowing. Kind of pretty.

He can see her sitting close to the window in the semi-dark. He can see the snow falling, and he can see the candle burning. He can even see himself there. Amy stands by the window. He is sitting in a chair. They are older. The room is warm, and the snow falls, and the scent pours off the candle. He is afraid of the warmth. He is afraid of her. He is afraid of himself. He wants to understand what it is that makes a man afraid of these good things, but he cannot.

She says his name.

Yes?

I really miss you. All day at work I thought how strange it will be coming home and you not here.

We'll be back before too long.

I know. I love you, she says. I can tell that, especially with you away.

Maybe he loves her, too. He can't tell. And he cannot say anything. The rain beats on his face, the wind blows across it.

I've got to go, he says. But I'll call tomorrow.

There's a box of tissues, a stool, and, built into the wall, a screen. He has deposited two tokens and watches the screen fill with flesh. He presses the channel selector button. Two girls. He pushes it again, and again. Two guys. Another indistinguishable smear of flesh. He thinks briefly of Amy and pushes the button again. A blonde girl and a guy whose face can't be seen.

He unbuttons his pants. He is not sure what he finds arousing about the scene. The girl is not pretty. The close-up shows that the hair around her asshole is slicked together with something. The pullback reveals that she doesn't look like she is having fun, though she grimaces and he can hear her grunting through the speaker. His cock is half hard and he strokes it without much expectation.

Then the door opens and a middle-aged Chinese man enters.

Hey, hey. He backs up, trying to put his cock back in his pants, but the Chinese man approaches him quickly, holding out an open palm.

Tokens, the Chinese man says with an accent, You want tokens?

No. His raises his hands as if to protect himself from a blow. He is much bigger than the Chinese man, but he is afraid of him.

The Chinese man nods and looks at the screen. He unbuttons his pants and exposes his own cock. Small and dark, it points upward at an angle. He strokes it, and the head slips in and out of the skin, the hole on the tip of it large and glistening.

You want? the Chinese man asks.

No. He has taken a step back. The Chinese man turns to him and stares at his face. With his free hand, the Chinese man reaches for his cock.

Wait, he says, stepping back again, but he is now against the wall. The Chinese man has seized the head of his cock and drops to his knees. He puts it in his mouth.

No, he says again weakly. The Chinese man sucks with a pressure unlike any he has felt before. Amy rarely sucks, and he doesn't know if he should ask it of her more often. One of her small breasts stands out of a spinning dark in his head. He looks at the screen but cannot tell what is going on there. He thinks in fragments of the night: the rat, the strip club, the sex shops, the rain and wind. He wishes he had gone back to the bar with Brian, where Brian and Brian's brother are now getting drunk in a relatively clean environment, probably talking about their old, clean memories of Montana. He feels a coldness throughout his body, even his balls. Only his cock is warm. He looks down and sees the Chinese man's face, with eyes closed and cheeks pulled in. He listens to the loud sucking noise the Chinese man makes and feels colder than before. He sees his face in the plastic of the screen gone blank. It looks out of proportion and awkward, like the face of disfigured stranger. He pushes against the shoulders of the Chinese man. The Chinese man looks up with small, bleary eyes.

Please, he says. Please stop.

He doesn't feel anything anymore. The Chinese man works a hand around to the back of his pants and then down them, through he struggles weakly to avoid the Chinese man's touch. The Chinese man begins to rub a finger over his asshole, and he says again, Please stop, but this time so quietly he can barely hear it himself. He squirms but feels he hasn't the power to get away. Please.

Here, the Chinese man says, pushing him back. Here, turn.

What?

Turn.

The Chinese man spins him and pushes him down so that has to take hold of the stool to stop from stumbling.

No, he says. He feels his pants and underwear yanked down to his knees. It is as if he is watching this happen on a screen to somebody else or some old self or some future self and feeling, distantly, the flush of it in his present body.

The Chinese man spits into the crack of his ass and he can feel it run down. Then the Chinese man fumbles for a moment. It hurts terribly at first. He cries out and tries to push the Chinese man away. The Chinese man leans into him, feeling heavy against his back, thrusting and breathing deeply. His asshole doesn't hurt anymore but feels almost numbed and he believes it is almost over.

Then the Chinese man pulls out suddenly. The Chinese man pushes him to kneeling and turns him halfway around and puts his cock in front of his face. Take, the Chinese man says. Take.

No, he answers, but without conviction. He can smell the shit. He wipes at the cock with his hand; it is smooth and wet. Then the Chinese man steps forward so the tip of the cock pushes against his closed lips. The Chinese man's hand goes to the back of his head and pushes it forward, so his lips open and the cock enters. It is foul in taste and feels small and very hard in his mouth. He wonders if he'll gag. The Chinese man thrusts in and out for perhaps a minute, before he stills and spurts hot come. Then he feels the pain of resistance in his jaw and ass. The Chinese man pulls his cock out, wipes it with a tissue, and leaves.

FUR BEARER

He was good-looking and quietly charming, and it happened
from time to time that he would meet a woman in a bar and
spend half the night with her. He believed he was outgrowing
these encounters—as if, at twenty-six, close to graduation, he
was experiencing a shift in consciousness—but he knew that
even if this were true, the process would be slow, and that
between its completion and now, he would still find himself
in a bar and later a bed with some woman or another.

The woman he met this night said she was a nurse and
worked at the nearby hospital. She had long hair, and her
nails and lips were bright. Her bust was large, her hips wide.
She looked like the kind of women he imagined all men
wanted and he told himself he would have her.

They ordered drinks.

She liked the indent in the muscle that showed in his jaw
line, she said, and his smile. He saw it himself in the mirror
behind the bar, the teeth closing, the lips pulling thin. His
mouth looked strong and sexy.

"You've got the face of a movie hero," she said.

He did not look at the mirror again. They made small,
sexy talk, touching each other on the elbow, staring into each
other's eyes, laughing quickly and quietly. He was bothered
occasionally by his overall vision of the uselessness of what
they worked toward. Each time it struck him like that and he
saw himself as playing a part he had outgrown, he took

another drink. After an hour, he paid the bill. When she took her coat from the check, he saw it was white fur.

"Nice, isn't it? It was a gift—the only good thing about that man was this gift," she said.

"It's real?"

"Yes. Do you have a problem with that?"

"I just think it's a waste," he said.

"Of what?"

"Of life. Of suffering."

She was looking at him skeptically.

"Are you a vegetarian?"

"No. I think of that as a sort of symbolic thing."

She gave a shrug of her shoulders and checked her hair in the reflection off of the glass door.

"But maybe someday I'll become one."

He thought of the pictures in the anti-fur brochure a friend had given him: various animals in traps, eyes bugged, skin sunken with dehydration. He tried to remember a description of the way these animals died or the number of certain animals it took to make a coat, but the information eluded him and seemed useless against her anyway. He didn't even know what kind of animals produced the fur from which her coat was made. He saw, for a flash, a white beast, some mixture of claw and saliva and slit eyes, snapping, snarling, spinning.

She put the coat on before looking at him again. Her eyes were a dark color of blue, the lashes black and matted together. She smelled of liquor and mint, and her lips were brighter yet. The world would not change in any way if he took a stand here and now. Nothing would breathe easier, be safer, suffer less, or live longer.

"It doesn't matter," he said, quietly. "You look fantastic. Should we go?"

"Good."

In her car he touched the coat. It felt like it was supposed to, soft and warm. He pressed down until he perceived the bone of her shoulder. She turned to smile at him, and he had a moment of repulsion. He withdrew his hand.

The car kept moving, past dark windows, stop signs, the dimly lit store fronts behind iron netting. He thought once or twice of saying something more—though the one-liners he'd learned from the pamphlet had slipped him—about her fur, her shallowness, but he said nothing. The fur should have made her ugly, but when he looked at her she was neither ugly nor pretty, and so he did not look at her anymore. The car continued to move, the inertia of it wearying him.

Later, when she lay back naked and seemed more obviously drunk than she had been in the living room, where they shared red wine and undressed, he felt alone with her body. He kissed her stomach and she writhed slightly. He put his palm flat against her lower abdomen and the pubic hair flattened out. Coils of it slipped up between his fingers. He kissed her again, below the belly button, where he could feel the hair brush against his face, hear a slight gurgle from her stomach, and smell the moisture from inside of her. Something in the heat of her body and the bristle of her hair stirred a place between his stomach and solar plexus. He felt numb and hungry, like a child who drifts in and out of sleep while continuing to eat.

He looked up at the woman's face and could not tell if her eyes were barely open or all the way closed and whether she was smiling. Her head was tilted up slightly and loose skin hung beneath her chin. A small expulsion of air came from her vagina, startling him. She lifted her head and looked at him with shamed eyes. She was no longer pretty. Still, he was going to take her. He was angry with himself that he would fuck her despite everything, and he was angry with her for the same reason.

He had the impulse to move up and strangle her. He could imagine crushing the coil of her windpipe; he could hear her choked breath, the silent pleading each small motion of her body would make, the sounds of tiny things popping.

Then he was alone in the living room. The numbness and focus was still on him. He went quickly across the room and to the closet, where he opened the door and carefully took the fur—still warm and soft—from its hanger. It was surprisingly heavy. Skinless bodies, muscle and blood and bone, whirled through his mind, black eyes in peeled faces of red and white—he heard a low, lost howling, the sound of a creature far away and forsaken.

He looked around. The light shone red, and from her dark room came a drift of stinking incense smoke. He stepped back from it, then turned and went quickly—and with a measure of joy—out the front door, into the night, carrying the fur still, as if it were a creature saved.

YOU MARRY A STRIPPER

You meet a stripper at the Laundromat. Dressed in paint-stained cut-off jeans and a sweatshirt, she has pulled her unwashed hair into a ponytail. She does not have makeup on her lips or around her eyes. You do not realize she is a stripper. You notice her panties—edged with lace, remarkably thin, remarkably small—and you believe in the mystery of her. Almost everything you will learn about her comes as a surprise to you.

She has a tired voice, and her eyes are fading, as if she's at the end of something. It's the middle of the day. She gives you change for your dollar. You stand there with the quarters waiting for the next thing.

How did it come, a marriage between you and this stripper? The coins, the fading eyes, the sunlight in the Laundromat windows. . . . One thing leads to another, and if you had to describe it, you would call it some kind of luck.

You do not want to believe all strippers are women somehow damaged. You want to believe your wife took to the business in search of a man like you. Patient but starving, she undressed night after night, waiting.

She has told you that the trick to her trade is to make every man believe the two of them have a secret relationship which transcends the club.

You have known the inside of strip bars, and you know now, with a kind of shame, the way you were dishonestly led to believe you were special so that you would leak dollar bills like sweet nothings onto the stage floor.

You wife is still a stripper, at least until you make manager at the department store and enough money for her to feel she can quit. She tells you specifically how it works. *I've got to make them believe that for that one dollar I might bring them home with me and fuck them . . . oh, but don't look like that, you're here, at home, you know they don't come here. It's just a trick . . .*

Though you are not certain what it is your wife means to take from you, you dream sometimes that she is working that trick on you now. You dream of sitting along the dance floor, the darkness cut by the lit faces of men and the bills of baseball caps and the glint of glasses, and your wife stepping high above all of it. Her blue eyes are frozen on the dollar you hold between your fingers. They are telling you that if that dollar drops, she will stay and be yours. It disappears before it reaches the counter, though, and her eyes move on.

In the early morning, before your day begins and after her night has ended, she lies beside you and dreams as well. She dreams she is naked in this same bed and above her sits a man whose face and body are cast in shadows. He works with his hands against his abdomen, and no matter how many times she has the dream, she always believes at first that he is masturbating. When he lets out his cry, she sees he has torn an opening around his navel, and everything inside him is pouring out. His guts fall on her bare stomach, her legs, her genitals. They both sit still for a few moments, and then he begins to scream and try to scoop the innards back, but they run between his fingers and fall back down on to her. She lies there beneath the mess of him, knowing she won't be able to rise and clean herself until the man is satisfied there is nothing of his he can take from her intact.

Is it you, faceless in her dreams? Is this what you intended when you married a woman who strips?

THE SPACE BETWEEN US

Little Red—whose name was given to him by his older brothers for his penchant for blushing heavily and for the remarkably small size of his head and limbs in proportion to his trunk—traveled down from Mobile to New Orleans on a kind of vacation from his job of selling tickets at the race track.

At about a quarter to midnight, Little Red picked up Carol, a young and somewhat frail-looking woman, who told him she'd worked the streets for the last half-year after relocating from a small town in Florida. She said those things rather quietly. She had nicely pale skin and he thought her teeth were beautifully bright. She complimented him on his manners and the delicate look of his hands, and he told her he liked what he perceived to be a genuine shyness in her. She took his hand in hers, and he lead the way.

Inside his hotel room she quickly undressed and reclined quietly on the bed, smiling nervously. Little Red appreciated that her professionalism was wrapped around a type of innocence rare not only in women of her trade, but in women in general. As he imagined himself to be a potential bright spot in what were probably rough lives, he always intended to be both gentle and satisfying with the prostitutes, but he determined to be especially so with Carol.

"Now just you relax there," he told her, unbuttoning his pants. "I'm going to go real easy and try to make you real happy."

He kneeled down on the foot of the bed and gently uncrossed her ankles. At first he thought her vagina was caught in a large shadow, but then realized it was not. The spread of darkness between her legs *was* the vagina, and it was absolutely huge. "Oh my," he whispered. He pushed back in surprise and surveyed her thin hips and the hard pouch of a belly and her nearly nonexistent breasts. He looked up and saw that she studied him with sad concern.

"Is it going to be okay?" she asked.

He sank back down and put his hands on her slightly plump thighs and pushed them farther apart. It was indeed the largest vagina he had ever seen. The lips were thick and long and hung heavily, reminding him of the flatbread treat called elephant ears he used to buy from vendors at the fair. The opening itself was at least four inches long and half as wide. The blackness, at which, in most women, a thin dark line only hinted, was, on this woman, a virtual ribbon. He had to close his eyes and open them again. Even the pee-hole, he noticed, using his fingers to push the lips slightly farther aside, looked like it would accept a finger. Only the clitoris and its hood were regularly sized.

"Oh my," he said. "Oh boy."

She lifted her head and fidgeted a bit.

"Well, shoot," he said, "I hate to say it, but I ain't going to do much for you with my. . . . Well, I mean you can see I'm not a big man, and anyhow, to be straight, I don't think that would make a difference. Can I ask you if you ever really get any feeling from anybody you been with?"

"I can't say for certain. I think I have. I certainly feel *something* down there when most men are going at it. It's kind of

J. ERIC MILLER

vague," she said, her eyes closing a little as if she were thinking about it. Then her eyes opened wide and she added in a high whisper, "Sometimes I wonder if the *man* feels anything. That's what I got to worry about, how it feels for *him*. I mean, most of them is awful nice. Every now and then a guy will walk out without doing anything, but even those guys will leave me the money. Everybody's pretty nice and I just worry about them, if they're getting anything."

Little Red thought about it for a little while. "I tell you something, Sugar. Tonight, this one night, I want you to forget all about whether or not the man—that would be me—feels anything, because I'll tell you a little secret. I feel it up here," he said, tapping his head. "Yeah, it don't matter much one way or the other if I feel you real tight or not. Shoot, maybe it don't matter at all. What I want to do? I want to make sure *you* feel something. Then we'll both be happy. I'll put my head to it."

She looked perplexed.

"Don't you fret. This I'm looking at as a challenge. So why don't you just lean back and close your eyes and I'll try to . . . move you."

Even as he spoke, he pushed softly against her chest so she sank flat to the bed. Then he kneeled down between her legs and stared at the pure openness of it while trying to formulate a plan.

"I'm going in for a closer look, don't get worried, okay?"

"Okay."

He put his face to it, and it seemed even larger than it had before, and he could not imagine it attached to a regularly sized woman like her, or any human being for that matter. It was, he thought with a fluttering in his stomach, the most mysterious hole in the world, the hole between himself and something beyond the bounds of the life he knew. *How to make the most of it? How to force feeling into that hole?* He swallowed hard and whistled low. Some almost unperceivable movement went through the mounds of flesh that clung around the base of the lips. He whistled again, more loudly, and this time the entire vagina reacted with something like a pucker which immediately collapsed.

He smiled and then blew as hard as he could. Though the breath itself did nothing, a shiver seemed to move up the vagina a moment later. "How we doing?"

"Mmm," she said. "You okay?"

"Sure thing."

"Really?"

"Sugar, really."

He moved forward, realizing he could not kiss it as a whole. He kissed each lip, sucking part of it into his mouth where it felt and tasted something like a cut of a portabella mushroom. Then he kissed the regularly sized clitoris and lapped at its regularly sized hood with the tip of his tongue. But after that? He went back to the lips and repeated the entire process again, realizing he was only trying to buy time. His methods were merely old standbys, and it was quite obvious that some much vaster effort would be necessary of him.

He sat back slightly and realized that at least she'd gotten both wetter, and, incredibly, wider.

"Mmm," she said again, but it rang a little false.

"Don't you worry," he assured her, feeling a slight sense of desperation. "I'll get it. You'll see."

On impulse, he thrust his face forward, so his nose sank all the way inside of her. He could feel the thick lips on either side of his face spreading out and trembling against his forehead. She gasped at the sudden motion, and he felt a movement of air against his face, as if something within her had drawn a breath. Sticking out his tongue, he begin to smear his entire face up and down, losing all sense of self, aware only of an overall feeling of slickness and steadily growing smell unlike any smell he knew, so strong it became less of a smell and more of a complete set of stimuli, almost visible, with a taste, and even, he thought, a sound. Encouraged, he tilted his head to use his chin.

When he pulled back to take a breath, he could see her vagina was giant and still growing bigger, blackness pulling out of flesh. Something vibrated in his solar plexus and he realized it was a call coming out from it to her and from within her to him. It was as if neither he nor she had let loose the original voice, but each was only an echo of the other. It was hypnotizing.

He rubbed a hand over his forehead and neck and found that he was soaked. He felt drunk, fatigued, lost.

She had begun to tremble. He could see it not only in the heavy lips, but in her thighs and the odd pouch of her belly. More importantly, the hood was gone, the clitoris fully exposed and erect. This grounded him. He was making her *feel* him. He stole a peek and saw her staring at the ceiling, panting.

The voice between them continued to reverberate.

He went back to smearing his face against her. Back and forth, up and down, blindly, almost forgetting what he was doing, as if his body—his head, more specifically—had been trained for this and needed no command or apparent purpose but would continue its work by pure instinct.

When a thought did cross his mind, it was the realization that he was resisting the impulse to lower his chin and work the crown of his skull against her. His body had been telling him for some time to do so, and yet a barely conscious part of his mind had been resisting. No more.

He lowered his face, held his breath, and began smearing his forehead and crown against the vastness and incredible wetness of her. *Ysssss,* he thought he heard her—it—say. Her legs rolled in his hands. Certainly she was caught on some rising wave. Certainly she was close to coming. Certainly. When he tried to pull back for a quick breath, he found his forehead suctioned against her or of its own volition refused to pull away. Furthermore, it seemed as if the whole of his head was being drawn steadily in, or perhaps it was that his head, commanded by the thing in his solar plexus, was pushing inward.

Either way, his flesh was tight against her flesh. And then there was the sound. He felt the sensation of a mass of flesh moving past him. His entire head, catching only for a moment at the ears, sunk inside of her, the lips slapping closed against his neck.

He was vaguely aware of what felt like things bursting all around and then: blackness.

He found he could not draw a breath. He found he could not call on his body to push against her and free his head, as if the two parts had become separated.

She was still now and very silent, and he himself was going still and silent as well.

CEREMONY

The dog pound is past the pig farms and slaughterhouse, out by the river and the sewage treatment plant. Thirty years ago, this northwestern city was the destination of many one-way tickets from some reservation or another. Ernie Cutfinger sometimes gathers people to partake of ceremonies his father, now dead, practiced in this same city when Ernie was a child. He doesn't know how far back the ceremonies go or how much they have been adapted. He doesn't know, either, how his version of his father's version would compare with ceremonies performed one hundred and fifty years ago, or even specifically what the ceremonies are supposed to do. He knows only that they exist.

He brings his boy, his girl, and his wife to the dog pound. It has been a year, and he counts on the fact that the women who work behind the counter do not remember him. They are tired and not vigilant, and they seem glad to see any dog go.

"Yeah, we want a young one. Not so small like this . . ." he bends over and puts his hands close to the floor, "but bigger, like this . . ." he lifts one hand a little.

The woman nods and says, "Why don't you look?"

Ernie and his boy walk the corridor lined with kennels. The girl waits with her mother on a bench by the front desk; their responsibilities—the skinning and the cooking—come later. The boy's eyes are wide and slip from side to side, noting gray and black paw pads split apart by the chain link doors; lolling tongues and wild eyes; an occasional still and staring dog; the curl of the back of one who will not turn. Some of the dogs knock their steel dishes of food around, and light brown pellets scatter out against the boy's shoes. He takes his father's belt loop in his fingers.

"Loud, huh?"

The boy nods.

Ernie squats. "This one." The dog, a half grown beagle mix, spins a circle, yipping. "This one?"

The boy frees his finger from the belt loop and puts it through the chain link. The dog stills, sniffs at the finger, then slopes out its tongue, and the boy pulls away.

"Like a snake, huh?"

The boy nods.

"Looks a little like that one that little boy Jimmy's got over at his house, don't it?"

Again, the boy nods.

"But it's always been this out here. I came with my father when I was like you." Ernie shows with his hand how little he once was. "This dog? He was always right here. Right behind this cage, waiting for us. All these dogs, they don't change. They just got their place in the order of things."

The dog has sunk to its haunches. Its eyes move from the boy's face to Ernie's face to the clasp that keeps its door closed. It gives a quick, excited yelp like an order and cocks its head. Ernie stands, nodding. "This one."

Slightly subdued, the dog sits in the back seat between the children. Absently, Ernie drums his fingers on the steering wheel, the sound of it punctuated by the rolling of a newly found lead pipe against the bare trunk. They go back past the sewage treatment plant, the slaughterhouse, the pig farms, and along the river, through this little stinking stretch of quasi-country in the middle of the urban sprawl.

The Owner knows something is wrong in his mall pet store. It seemed a good idea three years ago. He would sell puppies, kittens, exotic birds, reptiles, and fish. And he thinks he remembers good times, good business, a general feeling of happiness in the store. Each morning now, though, he finds the place is haunted, the employees jittery, he himself completely on edge, baffled, afraid. The customers sense it and stay away. The puppies and kittens begin to grow in the plastic cages, and he has to ship them to pounds and experimenters.

To make things worse, almost every morning he finds something dead or injured.

The chimpanzee grows more sullen by the day. They've turned his cage to face away from the doorway because he winces at the approach of pet store visitors. They've hung a full-sized poster of a different, smiling chimp so that people will know he is there.

Sometimes, looking in at the beast, the Owner wonders if he ought to just shoot it. He thinks absurd thoughts: he ought to come in here and shoot every living thing and be done with it. But not only does he not have a gun, he doesn't have the real will to do so.

His manager, a younger man named Reggie, is equally frustrated but more rational. "Something's going on here," he tells the Owner. "We should try to get a hold of it."

The Owner agrees, but neither of them has a plan to turn the business around. The Owner slips into memories which present the pet store as a place of joy. He smiles thinly, thinking of the time he framed and hung the first dollar spent there. He used to pass his afternoons in the aquarium room with the fish of all size and color. There were green fingernail slivers darting about, and sluggish silver and gold fists sitting heavy in the water, blinking their eyelids. *Don't tap the glass—for them it's equivalent to a gunshot being fired in your ear.* In tall, thin cylinders, he kept Japanese fighting fish. Teenage boys sometimes moved them one beside the other to see the fish lunge at each other and hit the glass and lunge again and hit the glass and finally learn and then sit staring with uncertainty.

Long ago, he created the joke which still stands: an aquarium with blue pebbles, plastic sea-leaves, water, and a filtration system. There were no fish, only colorless bubbles rising against the florescent, pinkish light. He'd hung a sign: *Invisible Fish—a rare form from Brazil.* He used to like to watch people stand before the tank looking to see what cannot be seen. They would peer in, squinting, and sometimes they would even tap, lightly, like a cap gun. Eventually they would straighten and frown.

Is this a joke? And at least a few times a day, somebody would see the flash of a tail, or the ridge of a back, or some other proof of the existence of the fish made visible in the odd combination of light and stone and bubble.

The pet store had been magical then, had been clean, had been promising. Or so he believes. But nobody stops anymore to see the invisible fish. Everything has gone sour.

The chimp knows the secret.

At night, the mall security guard tortures the pet store animals. He raises the steel curtain an hour or two before going in, so that parakeets will have by necessity given up on their panicked vigilance and gone back to sleep. Then he can creep in and knock them from their perches, watch them thump to the floor, scramble up in surprise, and look around stupidly, slowly blinking big black eyes, as if waking from the dream of a pet store to the reality of a jungle where they are prey.

But it has gone far beyond that. Now the security guard brings things from home: matches, rubber bands, a paring knife, darts. The chimp stays up at night, peering through screw holes in the back of his cage, seeing in collage the guard with the animals.

And in the morning, the Owner asks himself, Why have the two rats turned on this one, poking out his eyes? Where have the iguana's back feet gone? Why would the rabbit drown in such a shallow dish? How is it that the ferret's asshole has turned to blood?

The guard watches a turtle spin slowly in the break room microwave . . .

The Owner asks the morning employee if there weren't ten hamsters instead of nine . . .

The chimp knows that eventually the guard will come to hurt him. Occasionally, he tests his level of pain, pinching his arm, squeezing his testicles, but he cannot take very much. He rolls on the floor of his cage, trying to make himself small, covering his head with his arm. The guard flits through the room, suddenly swinging his baton into the parrot who has been teetering from side to side repeating, *Uh-ohh, uh-ohh, uh-ohhh . . .*

The Owner dreams. He sees an ark, a steady progression of animals from the forest. This is a good dream. But no, the trees are dead and a reek rises from them in a steam. The sun is hot and it will never rain in this dream. And inside his ark, the animals begin to scream.

The guard is working his way back, night by night. Burning, maiming, killing. Blood and death. He does not know that there is a chimp. He has not yet hurt a fish. This night, he finds himself peering into the invisible fish aquarium. Where are they?

He uses his flashlight, not sure he sees anything. He rolls up his sleeve and sticks his hand in the water.

The chimp hides his head.

The guard searches, hand darting this way and that, fingers curling and uncurling. He searches and searches, but never gets his hands on anything that feels like a fish.

They must be quick, wary . . .

Frustration grows in him like pain. He grabs the aquarium at its edges and pulls it from it shelf and drops it to the floor, where it shatters. The guard believes he can see flashes of the little fish as the water spreads thin and they suffocate. "That'll take care of you," he says.

Then he turns and sees the frightened chimp, so unexpected and so unlike anything in the pet store that the guard pokes his finger through the cage out of genuine curiosity. "Hey," he says.

Then the chimp does something he never imagined himself doing. He bites, quickly and hard.

"Goddamn," the guard says, pulling his hand away. "I'll get you later."

In the morning, Reggie the manager has figured it out. He tells the Owner, "The damn chimp has been getting out. How else would the aquarium get pulled down? Look, if he bends his fingers through there, he would maybe be able to pry open the cage. The little bastard."

It all dawns on the Owner: the chimp has been hurting the animals for some time now, has been leaving the odor of torture in the pet store, has ruined business and the goodness that once was. "That evil son of a bitch," the Owner says, gritting his teeth in anger and surprise and pain.

They go to the storeroom and make a plan.

"We'll kill him."

"But how? I don't have a gun. Do you have a gun?"

"No," Reggie says. "But I know, we'll wait till after closing. We'll bring him back here. You got something hard to hit him with? A tire iron?"

"Yeah," the Owner says. "Of course, in my car."

"Bring it in. We'll kill him."

The Owner thinks for a moment. Then he says, "He deserves it."

The chimp is glad for the touch of these men, though it also makes him nervous. He's never seen these two hurt the animals. Perhaps they will take him where the guard cannot get him. Even as he tries to imagine them into saviors he knows it cannot be so.

They put a cloth wrap around the whole of his head so that he cannot open his mouth very wide. Reggie lifts him out with leather gloves.

He wraps his arms around Reggie's neck, though it is only because he cannot think of what else to do.

"Careful," the Owner says. The face of the chimp is ugly and evil to him. "Don't look at me like that, you little son of a bitch."

The chimp makes a small sound, uncertain of what he wants it to mean.

"Shut up," the Owner tells him.

In the storeroom, the men set the chimp on a steel table. He sinks back to his haunches and looks up at them. They lift their tire irons.

"Should we just start hitting him?" the Owner asks, feeling a loss of sensation in his gut.

"That's what we got to do."

The chimp looks from face to face. He looks at the heavy metal objects in their hands, and he understands. He puts his elbows over his head and hunkers down. They strike blindly at first, breaking his arms, his ribs. He falls from the table and tries to scramble to standing. His leg is shattered. His head splits open. His brains spill out, and he thinks nothing more.

Reggie takes him into the woods and buries him.

The Owner dreams his terrible dreams of rotting corpses and the ark in the desert.

The guard does not properly clean the bite mark on his finger. By the time a week has passed, his hand is pus-swollen and stinks. The bite marks turn green and the skin begins to peel away. He takes to his bed and dreams fever dreams. His arm grows thick with poison and his hand dies, curling up. He wakes sometimes to the feel of the flesh along his arm and shoulder cracking open. When he tries to jerk away from the stench and the pain he finds he cannot move. He wishes for water and saviors but he knows that none will come.

FISH

I walked behind a wall of rock that cut between me and the ocean. I don't think I had a destination. Perhaps I was under the illusion that I could walk forever. It was cloudy and cool. A violent storm had passed the night before, and it soon began to rain again. I found a wide trail in the sand. It was smeared in places with blood and scales, as if a giant fish had been dragged there. There were handprints sometimes, also marked with blood.

I followed the trail until I came upon mermaid. She clawed for finger-holds on the rock wall. Her tail, three feet or so of gray scales which ended in the fork of a fish's fin, seemed to weigh her down in the soft sand. Her hair was long and sun-blond and tangled. Her torso was pressed against the side of the rock as she struggled to pull herself up it. Muscles constricted along her shoulders and back—shades of brown cut by the white lines of scars. She turned slightly and I could see there was a gash in her forehead and dried blood down the side of her face and neck. She had green eyes. I knew a woman with that color of green in her eyes.

I turned around. I saw my own footprints crisscrossing the trail she'd left dragging herself along the inside of the rock wall.

I looked again at the mermaid. Her entire torso shuddered as she collapsed against the beach. After a moment, she pushed herself up on her elbows. Then she froze, like an animal smelling danger. She turned to face me. Her mouth opened, but no noise came through it.

I went toward her. She clutched again at the rock. There was a murky smell. Her arms and face quivered. When I was close, she spun over completely so that her back was against the rock. She hissed at me, almost like a cat, and then she was perfectly still.

I touched her tail; it was firm and dry. She was still, but her pale lips parted and exposed dull-colored small teeth, some of which were broken. Her chin tilted back, causing thin cords to stand out on her neck. Her breasts were small and loose-hanging, with tiny nipples. I had an impulse to bring my hand up to them, but I did not follow it.

The end of her tail rose and fell slowly. It was torn in several places. The gaps had a gray, fleshy quality to them and showed blood just below the surface. I lunged when I saw that was about to react with the full force of her body.

We struggled. She struck at me with her hands and her elbows, tried to crash her forehead against me. Then she began to snap her teeth. Nothing hurt me and no solid thought passed through my mind. I eventually subdued her. She lay panting below me. I hefted her to my shoulder, where I squeezed her so tightly she lost her breath and could hardly move. Using my free arm for balance and pull, I climbed the rock wall. She tried to break free several times but there was no strength in the effort. I thought we'd fall backwards, or I would be forced to drop her, but we made it to the jagged crown of the rock. I walked across it and swung her from my shoulders, lowering her toward the ground by her arms. She became too heavy and I let her fall.

Immediately, she began dragging herself across the beach toward the ocean, ten yards away. I suddenly wanted to shout to her, to make her respond to me in some way. I dropped to the sand and walked toward her. She let out a cry when I put my hands on her tail. I twisted it so that she turned onto her back. She rose, her eyes very dark, and snapped at me with her mouth. I slapped her across the face, though I didn't intend to. She sank back to the sand. My hand felt like it was burning. Fresh blood ran from her forehead. She lay still, her arms flung upward, laying in the tangle of her hair.

I tried to think of something to say. Lightning flashed; I counted two seconds before the thunder sounded. The rain fell harder. There were two small fins on either side of her tail. A little more than halfway down, there was another fin in the middle, and just below that was an opening. Her head was tipped back, her eyes on the water. Raindrops splashed on the surface of her cheeks. I put a hand on her stomach. She had the kind of scars there that I associate with pregnancy. Her belly was trembling slightly. I shifted forward so I was over her. Her mouth was barely open, as if she had just uttered a word.

I lowered my face to hers, and then my torso. I felt her breasts flatten beneath my chest. The breath from her nose spread across my face, and I kissed her gently on her cold, salty mouth. I kissed her again, thinking of the things which must have passed through her mouth—saltwater and seaweed and fish. My mouth opened hers and I forced my tongue inside of her lips. There was a taste I didn't recognize. I imagined the dark places in the water beneath the storm— the calm places jellyfish and sharks and other creatures silently glided, places through which ships must have sunk, for minutes, or hours, maybe even days, bubbles tumbling up from them and bursting against the surface.

I felt my hands on the muscles of her back, kneading them. A sudden shame passed over me, and I rose.

She lay there, and I was afraid I had frozen her in that position. Then she slowly turned and pulled herself into the water. She was soon in up over her elbows, then her torso. Her head was overcome by a wave. Her tail lifted and slapped against the water and she was gone.

MERCY KILLER II

Perhaps a cat had gotten to the pigeon. It lay in the sunlight on a sidewalk behind the campus church, several gashes across its head. It looked dead, except for the slight rising and falling of its back as it breathed. Sorry to have been the one to notice it, he squatted beside the bird and stared. Blood ran into the pigeon's upturned eye, and it was unable to blink away the pool that had formed there. The tip of its gray tongue jutted from its beak and moved slightly. It was a hot day and he considered bringing the bird water, but it probably couldn't drink. It was going to die slowly and in pain.

He could stand least of all the blood-covered eye and the blackness that shone through, and the question of whether or not it was looking at him.

After a while he rose. He went to the library, which was always kept soothingly cool. On the way, he made a deal with himself. He checked out a book he needed for a class project. Then he went back to see if the pigeon had died. It hadn't. Apparently it had had some fit of movement, for one of its wings was folded at an odd angle beneath it. He looked around for anybody, but he and the pigeon were alone. The windows on the surrounding brick buildings that stood all around reflected the sun.

"I made a deal," he said.

He looked around for a large stone or some wooden debris with which to kill the bird. It seemed an odd and perhaps impossible thing to accomplish. He remembered that as a boy he'd killed several birds with his pellet rifle, and that each of these killings had been followed by a secret burial. He had no simple weapon so.

It was a pretty, well-kept campus, and he walked past the church and across the lawn in search of something solid. He went along slowly, peering beneath trees and into the shadows cast by buildings but found nothing. Eventually, he turned back toward the pigeon, saying as he went, "Let it be dead."

It wasn't. Again, it had moved. Now its head was tucked down against its body. One of the wings lifted and fell and lifted again. It struck him that his car was in the nearby lot. The realization was both frightening and relieving. He picked up the pigeon. It struggled against his hand until he squeezed his fingers over its wings so that it could not move them. Its head lolled and it did not resist any longer. He felt its heart going so fast that one beat was almost indistinguishable from the next.

"I'm sorry, sorry, sorry . . ." he repeated.

He set it down close to the front tire. It flapped one wing, moved in a half circle, and then stilled. Turning away from the pigeon, he had the feeling that the most difficult part was already behind him, as if in holding the bird tightly he had faced the responsibility of his choice, and in so doing had set something in motion he no longer had to force himself to finish because the momentum of it would see him through. He did not look at the pigeon again, but got in his car and backed up and drove forward so that the tire was directly over the bird. "Jesus," he said, and then tapped on the gas. The car jerked and he tapped harder and felt the slight lift of the car going over the pigeon's body.

Dazed, he got out of the car and started back toward the library. He'd misplaced his book, but he couldn't remember if he'd put it down when he picked up the bird, or sometime earlier. It was in the grass by the church, and he took it, planning to go back to the library and read there. But he couldn't. The thing between him and the pigeon wasn't over. He had to see it dead.

When he got back to his car, he could only find a smear of blood and feathers. As he rose from his crouch, a cry startled him. Though half of its body appeared to be crushed, the pigeon was now standing several feet away on a patch of grass in front of the car. The pigeon looked larger than it had before—being run over had elongated its body, but there was also a puffiness to the head, so that it appeared the size of a fist. It cried out again and hopped in his direction. He stumbled back, and the pigeon, moving toward him in a broken way, tumbled and stilled, except for one foot which kicked out. The claw trembled as the crushed talons appeared to try to separate themselves. The crying began again.

"Jesus," he said. He got in the car and pulled backward. He drove forward more carefully this time, and, opening his door and leaning out, he confirmed that the pigeon's head was in the shadow of the tire. He accelerated before the bird could move. The explosion of the skull was much louder than he expected. It was like a gunshot, echoing throughout the campus which, otherwise, was perfectly silent.

He half-fell out of the car and started at almost a run away from the parking lot. The book was missing again, but he didn't care. Back inside the library, he sank into a couch and felt the coolness of the room and smelled the books which made the place seem familiar, but he could not calm himself. His heart was beating hard and there was something wrong in his stomach. He wanted to make contact with some passing face, but he could not raise his eyes to any of them. He realized, with an incredible sense of weariness, that he had to go back. He had to see the bird and understand the explosion that still echoed in his ears.

Now the size of a small dog, the pigeon stood on the front bumper of his car. Its head was a flattened mat of blood and bone and stiffened feathers, its burst eyes black smears, its beak only a jagged stub. It appeared somehow more vigilant than it had been before. It leapt from the front bumper onto the hood of the car and grotesquely struggled for balance.

"You can't be," he said. The pigeon turned toward him. Puffing itself up, it let out a loud squawk. He almost ran away. The broken wing rose awkwardly and shook. He looked up into the windows of a brick building for a witness, but there was no one. When he looked again, he saw the bird shit, a large, bloody goop, onto the hood of the car. Then it turned and took several steps, jerking its head in an imitation of the bobbing fashion with which pigeons move, as if it meant to be now what it once was.

"You can't," he said.

It ran itself into the windshield, making a dull splattering sound, and tumbled backwards. Crying out again, it rose and repeated the process, this time leaving a small nick in the glass and made a stain of black blood and some kind of viscera. Moving more quickly each time, it repeated the process again, and then again.

He went as if by instinct to the car. He opened the back door and dug under the seat for the tire iron. Now he was moving quickly. When he approached the pigeon, it stopped, stared up at him, and let out a cry that he could feel in his chest. He swung the tire iron and knocked the pigeon off the car, over the edge of the parking lot, and onto the lawn. He ran to it and beat it until his arms were tired and the pigeon had been torn into so many pieces there appeared to be barely anything left of it. He lost himself in the beating and only came fully conscious again when he was walking back toward the library. He could not remember what he had done with the tire iron or exactly when or why he'd stopped hitting what was left of the pigeon. He felt numb and oddly at ease.

Inside, he rested again on the couch. His stomach did not feel sick, but hard, as if it was made entirely of muscle. People walked by, but he did not know their faces, or care. He sat in a daze that was like a dreamless sleep. When he finally had a thought again, it was simply that his day was over. The classes he was supposed to attend in the afternoon did not exist. It was time to go home.

The windshield of his car had been shattered. The hood was deeply scraped and dented, as if it had been beaten by a baseball bat. He looked for the pigeon. It stood watching him from the top of the nearest brick building. It appeared as big as a five-year-old child, and everything on it was mangled. For a moment, it was perfectly still, and he believed that none of what had happened since he found the pigeon was real. Then a tremble ran through it. He meant to move in some type of response, but he could not. It reeled down, falling like a huge, wind-broken kite. The weight of the blow knocked him to the ground, and he felt the talons sink into his chest and grip.

"Off," he tried to scream at the bird, but the word only came in a moan.

It shit again, the stink of it overwhelming, and its heat against his belly and groin was almost unbearable. He tried to roll from beneath the pigeon, but he could not. "I'll kill you," he said, but he knew, even as he spoke, he wouldn't. It raised its broken head on its broken neck and wailed, not like a bird, but like a human, as if his own voice was rising up through the talons that were embedded in his muscle, coming up through the twisted body of the pigeon and out its shattered beak.

TWO JOGGERS

Hank and Jerry drove all night and stopped in the early morning for breakfast at Denny's. Afterwards, they drove a ways out of town to a turnoff to dirt road Hank had scouted two months before. They parked just off the highway, away from the turnoff. Hank wrapped the rifle in a military blanket because nothing was in season in the middle of summer. It was still fairly conspicuous, and as they moved through the trees Hank whispered to Jerry, "Watch out."

Jerry nodded and looked around. He was twenty and had fallen in with Hank a year ago. He'd gone out with Hank three times and had learned a lot. Hank had been doing this sort of thing for ten years or so. He had a trimmed beard and almost always wore mirrored sunglasses. "HUNTER" was tattooed across his chest. Jerry was thinking about getting one himself.

Jerry pointed to some deer droppings. They were black and fairly dried out. "My daddy used to take me poaching when I was a kid," Hank said. "Said it was no fun and not right to shoot something in season."

Alongside the road ran a stream and they walked on its bank. Jerry tried to match Hank's long, purposeful strides. After a mile or so they climbed a short hill that overlooked the road.

Hank unwrapped the rifle and checked its sights. "There will be some movement around here," he said.

"You sure?"

Hank looked at Jerry for two or three seconds but did not answer. Then he went back to checking the rifle.

"You think anybody will hear the shot?"

"Maybe. We're about five miles from the nearest housing development, though. By the time anybody comes to check it out, if anybody does, we'll be back in the truck and gone."

"I guess we got to be quick though."

Again Hank did not answer. He rolled his head around and cleared his throat. It was growing warmer. Jerry wanted to keep as still as Hank was, but he found it hard. He caught himself breaking off twigs and breaking those twigs into pieces and digging into the dirt with his boots. Eventually he took out the knife and studied its blade. The night before Hank had sharpened it into a perfect edge.

"Listen," Hank said.

Jerry looked up and cocked his head to the side. Then he heard the sound of feet falling on the road below. Soon, a man in blue shorts and a blue baseball cap appeared. He was jogging at a quick pace. Jerry looked at Hank to see what he would do, but Hank watched the man passively. After the man had gone, Jerry said, "Can I hold the rifle?"

Hank looked at Jerry skeptically. "Do you think you're ready for that?"

"You said this time I could make the shot maybe."

"That's true. I said maybe."

A moment passed before Hank handed Jerry the rifle. "All right," Hank said. "But you better be ready. And you better not pause, even for a second."

"I won't."

They waited another quarter of an hour. Jerry shifted the rifle from hand to hand and sighted it against several rock formations and tree branches. He felt like nothing more was going to happen and a bitter disappointment grew in him.

Then he saw that Hank had gone perfectly still and focused on the bend in the road below. After a moment, she came into view. She had been moving fairly quickly but slowed almost to a walk now and then stopped all together, as if she sensed danger. She was not that close to them but Jerry thought he could see her nostrils flare.

"Come on," Hank hissed.

Jerry had practiced it with Hank many times, and now he let that training take over. He swung the rifle to his shoulder, closed one eye, sighted the rifle to a place several inches above her head, and put his finger to the trigger. He did not pause. He squeezed, as he'd been taught, and the rifle fired. She fell.

Jerry could not move for a second. Harry was already up and moving down the hill. He turned and said, "Give me the knife."

Jerry nodded and rose. He wrapped the rifle in the blanket and took the knife out of the sheath, then jogged to catch up to Hank and hand him the knife. She lay across the path, half of her head shattered. One of her dull brown eyes was visible, and looking at it, Jerry felt a hot sensation in his stomach. Hank knelt down and worked quickly, drawing the knife from her throat down her torso and belly. He spread the ribs, reached through them, and pulled free the heart. Then he cut around it with the knife so that he could remove it entirely. He dug a plastic bag from his pocket and put the heart inside of it.

"You're going to eat of this one," Hank said. "Now that you're making the kill you've got to partake."

"I don't know," Jerry said. He knew that Hank felt that what they did was all tied up in the act of eating the heart, but it was different for Jerry. For him the pleasure was in the build-up. He enjoyed the long drive from their hometown to wherever they went to make the kill. He liked to listen to Hank tell stories about other hunts and other times of his life. He liked it that they always had breakfast just after dawn, the way the food woke them up and fortified them for the day. He enjoyed, too, the walk through the woods and the wait, which always seemed to go on longer than he could stand. Then there was a shot, loud and heavy, and a momentary sense of release. Whatever happened after that fell into a sort of dead space.

"Come on," Hank said. "Move your ass. We got to get back to the truck."

Jerry stood up. Hank was already moving quickly down the road. Jerry looked again at her, the blood from her wound pooling in the dirt beneath her head, her tongue stuck out between her teeth. He looked at the slit Hank had made in her and the way her guts could be seen still quivering inside. He didn't now what he felt then, but he decided that if Hank found it important to eat the heart it must be, and he would try it.

IN THE PRIDE OF LIONS

I never would have thought to take his woman when I knew him years ago. He was more successful than the rest of us and was something of a leader. "Listen," he said, "you must do like me. Like a lion. The lion knows it is a game of numbers. Keep pouncing until you bring one down. Get fed." I did not like the analogy because I do not eat meat. And never mind that in lion culture, it is the female who hunts.

He was strong, handsome, had a golden mane, and there was always the smell of some woman opened up in his small one-room apartment.

But now, after returning to this city, I find him older. His hair is short and thinned, the cut of his body blurred by fat, his jowls soft, his brilliant teeth dulled. He is not a hunter anymore. He has only one woman, and she is made all of bones, with red, tangled hair. It is that she belongs to him that makes her worthy. I sit in their living room. She crosses and uncrosses her legs, her calves overly bent. I study her lips, her throat. I sniff for the scent of her, but in this room there are old cigarettes and days and days of unopened windows.

She has heard nothing about me from him. She asks me why I left and why I have returned. I tell her that I am moving from the city of my graduate program to the city of my new job, and visiting this old haunt along the way.

There is a nature program on the television. Wild dogs in Australia or Africa. One of them is a loner and clearly starving. He comes across three or four begrudgingly sharing a carcass. The loner lopes up and sniffs his way toward the meat, but the others snarl and then leap, snapping at him. He limps away, makes a half circle, is chased again, and then turns and walks into the yellow grass. There he stands with his tongue hanging and his ribs shaking, watching the others eat.

"That's very sad," I say. "They should have shot him. Or fed him. Those people making the video."

"Typical of you," my old friend says, "not wanting to let nature be what it is." He smiles at the girl and she appears to study me.

I think of our old arguments about eating meat and decide against having one of them now. I look again at the woman and then at my old friend, and I think: *In the natural world, somebody bigger than you and stronger than you would take her from you, whether she wanted him to or not. That's how it works, in nature.*

The narrator tells us it is a hard world. We watch shots of animals starved or killed in long grass, at the edges of muddy water holes.

"Well," my old friend says, "let's go."

We used to play ball. He was quicker and stronger than me, with a more natural eye for the basket. We walk down to the courts. His eyes are tired. He is not happy to see me. But walking and dribbling the ball, he smiles. He rolls it in his hand, studies its surface. I think of his woman.

I imagine that from the window she watches us to the corner. "She wants to have a baby," he says.

"She's told you?"

"No. I just know it. She's up to it, to get a baby."

He takes off his shirt and makes a few practice shots. I wait. He's gained soft weight. I used to be nervous playing, but I feel good now. I sense an inevitability to this game. It begins and I see right away that his grace is gone.

He is off-balance. His tits bounce, his underarms wiggle. I win the first game easily, and the second. He is frustrated. "Christ," he says. "I haven't been playing for a while."

Though he is no longer made of muscle, he is still much bigger than I, and he begins to push his weight into me. Once, drunk, we almost fought, and I was afraid because I knew from the pressure he applied leaning into me that he would be able to hurt me. He is trying to intimidate me in that way now, but it doesn't work. I shift away. He stumbles, nearly falls, and I score. Soon he throws elbows, brings up knees, and I use these mis-motions to my advantage, though, now and then, a shock of blackness rocks my head. Sometimes he knocks me down. Sometimes he falls.

Regardless, I win again and again. I want to stop, but he refuses.

"One more," he keeps saying.

We're both scraped in several places, sweaty. His breath is rank, his eyes wild. At some point, he tries to put an elbow in my gut and misses. I spin. He stumbles a few steps. His back is to me. It is instinct which makes me leap at the exposure and bring him down. He rolls and I can feel the old strength of him, but I am centered and let him shift beneath me without bucking me. Then I begin to strike into his face and throat. My hands are numb; his face is bloody, his eyes grow dim. I leave him moaning.

As I approach his apartment, the adrenaline keeps my muscles and nerves quivering. I know what I am supposed to do. I climb the stairs, dark and smelling of old water. Her eyes widen as I come through the door, but she doesn't move otherwise, staring at me from under the wild of her red hair. A newscaster talks on the television.

The sundress she wears is thin, wavery, nothing. I can feel the bone through her arms, a strong bone, I think, lifting her to meet me. Her hands curl on my elbows and her nails are sharp. If she fights, I imagine she will hurt me, but in the end, I will win.

J. ERIC MILLER

PRINCE PUSSER TAREN

Kristy, Kathy, Katie? I can't remember her exact name. She's gone to steal a condom from her roommate's medicine cabinet, and I'm worried about getting a hard-on. Perhaps it's because I'm tired. In the mirror on her wall, my shoulders are hunched as if I'm older than my father, two years dead, ever was. I remember having read that long ago, when a monk's apprentice had an erection, he was forced to stand facing a wall and the monk would kick the boy in the ass until the erection was gone.

"Hey," I ask the reflection, "what made you so worn out? When she comes back, you come to life. Okay?"

And get a hard-on.

Girls get the mothering instinct with me, maybe because I never knew my own. Maybe they sense—though I don't know for certain their sense is right—that I'm looking for something maternal. But I'm too old to be babysat or breast-fed, so they bring me to their homes, their rooms, undress me, undress for me. I like most girls' rooms. I like to look around and see their personal things. What I've started to think about tonight, though, is my own room, large and bare, a place to which I never bring any girls. I don't know why I'm tired or what I'm tired of, but thinking of my room only makes it worse.

I think about a girl I used to know: Amy King. When I was in fifth grade, she freed me from a slide to which a guy named Dean McCarty had tied me with a jump rope during recess.

Before I saw Amy walking past Dean and toward me, I imagined I'd be there until dusk, and then my father would call the police. To his shame, they'd find me not kidnapped, murdered, or otherwise reasonably lost, but merely bullied. Amy King walked past Dean McCarty and he didn't even try to stop her. The playground was hers, certainly not mine, not even Dean's. Her fingers on the knots were magically long.

We became kind of friends, Amy and I.

I wonder where she is now. She was raped graduation night, in the back seat of a car, by three or four guys I imagine to be just like Dean McCarty. I really didn't know her very well by that time. I wonder if her fingers are still long and if she still owns the places into which she walks the way she owned the playground.

But I don't want to think about her now. I need to think about the girl—who I can hear rummaging somewhere in the house—and what we'll do and how I'll like it. I want to think of something that will give me a hard-on.

Getting one hasn't been a problem for me in the past. In fact, I can usually keep one for a long time. My method to slow ejaculation is to think of cartoon characters: Bugs Bunny pulling a rug out from under Yosemite Sam; Wile E. Coyote suspended in mid-air; sometimes Elmer Fudd pointing his pink-tipped finger at me, saying "Swoe down, dwon't cwum." I can go on and on, till I am asked to stop, or till I'm exhausted. Then I like to watch the woman put back on her panties. I like to leave her in her bed beneath the covers with a kiss. I like to skip across her lawn in the cool night air, to look back at her dark window before opening my car door.

What is her name? It is spelled with a "K," she told me. I hear her coming down the hallway. In two hours, I'll be driving back to the home I've shared with Jen since our father died. Perhaps she will be up. Jen is simple in a beautiful way.

She is full grown, but with the innocence of a child. It occurs to me that she likes living better than the rest of us do.

The ghost of a lisp you can hear when she speaks now was in full bloom when she was a child. Knowing my father's impatience with any type of clutter, she used to whisper after each meal: *Push your chair in.* It sounded like: *Pusser Taren.* I believed it was the name of a prince, and that she was secretly and continually reminding me that he was going to arrive some time soon and take us to a magic place. I guess I waited for that the way other people wait for UFOs or lottery winnings.

The girl returns. "Hey, I found one." It dangles from her fingers. I've forgotten to unslouch, but she doesn't seem to notice.

Sitting beside me, she says, "Do you need a little help?"

"I'm just tired."

She takes my dick in her fingers. Then her head sinks toward my lap. Warm and soft, like everything else in here. I've been from room to room in this city, from girl to girl. I connect the dots and look at them from high above—a series of lights, a picture trying to complete itself. I like the drive home. The stars and clouds. The radio voices. I like it all. Jen and I drink soda and play cards most evenings, even if I get back late. I'd like to be home with her now, though the fuck and the rest of it is not yet behind me.

A friend of mine had a theory. He said that we will move beyond everything we like. It was his idea that we've got a certain amount of ability to feel genuinely good about the things which please us, and that if we indulge them long enough, one day we will have used it all up. I think of that now. Maybe I can just get up and leave. I think about Amy King again. I picture the back seat of a car, torn up and dirty, and a bunch of guys half undressing and then dressing. I think of monks kicking against my ass. I think of Prince Pusser Taren, a cartoon drawing of a young man, his face wrinkled with uncertainty at what he witnesses as he peers at me.

None of it works. I get hard.

THE MOTIONS

They made the date when she and her sorority sisters were slumming in the kind of a hole of a bar he'd been frequenting for several years. She was quite drunk and he was drunk enough to feel the type of lightness that made everything, even her, seem possible. He was not sure if the want was genuine, but it seemed like the right thing to feel. Now he was not drunk, and he felt out of place in the Greek Row neighborhood, with the three-story homes full of students in the prime of their lives. He had gone to the nearby university, but that was five years ago, and it seemed longer than that. Maybe in the bar he looked like a college student to her, and not a man who was living off a disability settlement from UPS.

She'd certainly see his age now. She would recognize the secret of dirt about him, of which he was aware but about which he had no specific knowledge. To take anything from her now would require more lies and trickery than he could muster. The apple he brought as a gift was too small and spotted, and he was early.

A girl in a sweatshirt and jeans answered the door. "Hello?"

"Is Megan here? I'm Alex, I'm supposed to . . ."

The girl turned and yelled Megan's name and his up the stairs.

After a moment, a girl in a bathrobe appeared at the top of the stairs, her hair wet and a comb in her hand. After another moment, he realized it was Megan. She seemed to study him and then gave a little wave.

"You're early. We had a house meeting and it got out late . . ."

He couldn't tell from her tone if she was annoyed with him or with the meeting going late.

Everything was wrong. He didn't want anything from this girl. He couldn't get anything from this girl even if he did want it. Why was he pretending he did?

He stepped back, saying, "My fault. I'll come back in half an hour."

A few blocks away, he stood at the left field fence of a base-ball diamond. It was overhung by huge lights that made the grass seem to glow and even the fine powder and dirt appear artificial. There were a few adults sitting in the metal bleach-ers on the other side of the field. A dozen boys, probably eleven or twelve years old, were spread across the field, with one in the batter's box, and one at the plate. Two grown men, each wearing a red wind-breaker and cap, stood at the mound, feeding day-glo orange balls into a machine that shot them out with a pop. The orange of the ball dulled in flight. Alex watched for a while as the kids rotated around the field. Every now and then, one of them would get a good hit on the ball and it would sail past the focus of the light into the dark-ness and thump down somewhere in the grass beyond.

A tall batter with startlingly big eyes came to the plate and started kicking into the dirt. There was something, perhaps a type of grace, about the way the boy moved that caused Alex to lean into the fence to see him better. The batter used his foot to build a little hill in the dirt.

"Come on, we haven't got much more time," one of the men on the mound said.

The other man had stepped off of it and was moving toward third base.

"Do you want me to break my ankle?" the kid called out.

There was a richness to his voice, as if he were a boy that not only played ball, but sang in the choir. Alex waited for the boy to say something more.

The man who had left the mound now reached the fence and stood a little way down from Alex.

There was the popping sound at ten second intervals, and the batter hit each of the balls, so that there was also the metal ding of the bat. Alex tried to find one of the balls in the sky, but he couldn't. The boy's arms were deeply tanned, almost golden, and his face, with those large eyes, was completely at ease in its concentration. Though he couldn't see them from this distance, Alex imagined that smooth lines of muscle stood out on the boy's forearms. Alex tried to remember that once he had been a boy. It seemed an impossibility. He could not recall his body, his thoughts, what it was he desired when he was that young. Was he ever so beautiful? The boy's hair was deeply blond, and even from this distance, Alex could see how it curled from under the red helmet and stood out against it. Alex leaned in even further, trying to see the face in detail, the color of the large eyes, the composure of the lips, the quality of the skin.

"Okay, go on this one," the man on the mound said. "We're almost out of time."

"Do you have a son on the team?" Alex was startled to see the other man so close.

The boy hit the ball and began running so fast toward first base he lost his helmet. Alex longed to study the stride, but the man was looking into his face in a way that made Alex step back.

"No. I'm not . . ." Alex couldn't imagine that he looked old enough to be the father of any of these boys.

The man took another step to the side so that he could lean forward, taking possession of the place Alex had just occupied.

The boy was now of the second base. Putting his hands on his hips, he glanced around him with a kind of confident nonchalance from which Alex had to force himself to look away. The man's mouth opened as if he meant to say something more, but Alex turned and begin walking along the outfield fence.

The other man flicked a switch on the machine and yelled for everybody to come in. Alex listened to their voices, high and excited, but he could not pick out the sound of the last batter. Perhaps the boy was silent now. He did not dare look again.

By the time Alex reached the first corner of the field, they were all huddled together by the dugout. He stopped again and watched the grownups coming down from the bleachers and cars pulling into the lot. He was too far away to tell one boy from the other, though he looked before continuing on. The boys walked toward their cars, and it was not long before the parking lot was empty again. He'd not been able to find that last batter, the tall boy with the blond hair and rich voice.

He wondered if it was time to go back and get Megan. He felt tired and absolutely uncertain of his desire to put forth any effort as it related to the girl. What had he come for then? Why had he zoned in on her in the first place? Charmed her, collected her number, done all the things he'd been taught by older friends and television and songs to want to do and to do.

He continued down the fence, passing first base now and working toward the dugout. "I can do it," he said out loud. "I should."

And then he believed it. He believed he could not only lie about where he was in life, but who he was. He could make her believe that he was good, even, worthy, convince her that he was the holder of some kind of magic of which she should want to partake. She could be made to not only accept him, but to want him, and then he could have her.

He tried to picture her face; he tried to remember her body. But there was nothing in his mind of her. There was an opening in the fence and he stood in it. He could see a ball on the grass, just at the edge of a circle of light. It was fifteen or twenty steps away. The field was absolutely silent, and it was hard to imagine that boys had been there hitting balls and calling out. Still, there was the evidence, something they'd forgotten or lost.

He thought of that ball later, as Megan worked her hand back and forth on his cock in the front seat of his car. He'd stood for a long time staring at the dusty orange lump. He wanted to pick it up, but he couldn't bring himself to step onto the green grass, which looked too perfect and tender for the likes of him. He'd looked into the light, which was blinding when directly confronted, and then back down at the ball, spots running through her eyes. Then the lights shut down.

He closed his eyes now and then opened them. He looked down, where his pants were open and his shirt tails pulled away from each other, forming a giant mouth. His legs and belly appeared thick and discolored. His pubic hair was tangled and grotesque and he had to turn away. Her hand began moving faster, and he had the impulse to grip her wrist and force her away from him. He tried to remember the blurred faces of any of the boys he'd seen on the field, but he could not. He tried to recall the last batter, his stance, the bend of his knees, any small detail, but none came. She jerked him harder still.

ROPHYNOL

There's a hotel on the south side of the city. It's been used this way before.

At eleven in the morning, the man wakes up naked save for his socks and wedding ring. He finds himself nauseous; his face burns; and his wrists and ankles ache. A dried substance mats his belly. The room is void of personal effects. His clothes are gone; everything is gone. The open mouth of his drink from the night before stands out in his mind, and he lets out a low wail.

The three women sat in the corner, where they could see everybody who came in. They picked him almost absently. Sheila went to him. She tried to draw him in with her smile, but he seemed distant. She told him her name.

He nodded.

Eleanor rose and approached the bar. Though the man had not turned fully away from his drink, she let the two tablets fall and dissolve in his gin and tonic as she leaned over to order a beer. From the corner, Barbara smiled a mean smile.

He was well-dressed, a bit pudgy, and had a pretty face. The man was in the bar for a reason, even if he didn't know it.

"Have you had a long day?" Sheila asked.

He shrugged, lifted his drink, drank from it, and then set it down. "I suppose."

"My friends and I saw you and I made the bet that you're a lawyer."

"No, an office manager. Not a lawyer." He smiled a little, and on the other side of him, Eleanor paid for her beer, sipped from it, and smiled as well. He noticed her, and his smile thinned a little, but then his expression seemed to relax and he drank. After a few moments, his face paled. He drank again as if to clear his head.

Shelia looked around the bar as if she didn't notice.

He tried to tap her but missed. "Something's wrong," he said, but his words were slurred and color continued to run from his face. "What's it from me?" he asked, and then his eyes begin to swim as if he were searching for the sense in what he had just uttered.

"I don't know," Sheila murmured. Then she said, more loudly, "Would you like to sit down with us?"

He shook his head. His face was now turning quickly from ashen to bright red. "No. I've to home soon . . ." Both women watched him. In the corner, Barbara smiled even more meanly. The man said, "I don't feel . . ."

He tried to rise but had trouble. Sheila took an arm and Eleanor the other, and they helped him. Barbara joined them.

He giggled once in the car, and Barbara and Sheila took turns kissing him on the mouth as Eleanor watched in the rearview mirror. Sheila unbuttoned her blouse and pulled her breast free of the bra and pushed his head down to it so that his lips rested against the nipple, and he seemed to suck there. She murmured as she had done in the bar, and Barbara flicked her fingertip against the man's earlobe, then turned away.

He was out cold in the hotel room, but, after they undressed him, they tied him anyway. Eleanor set up the video camera. Sheila lifted his limp penis between her fingers and kissed it.

"Look at me," Eleanor said quietly, and Sheila turned toward the camera, smiled, and kissed the penis again. Barbara wiggled the fat on his belly, then bit sharply into it. Sheila was now sucking hard against his penis, and it began to grow. "See?" she said.

Eleanor answered, "He'll tell himself tomorrow he never wanted this, but his cock knows, doesn't it?"

Barbara stuffed her panties in the man's mouth, studied his face, frowned, and then took them out again. She pulled up her skirt and squatted over his face, smearing her vagina and anus against his still lips.

His penis was fully erect, short but thick, and Sheila drove her head up and down on it, letting out thin, hungry whimpers. Barbara began moving furiously against his face, and he began to turn his head from one side to the other and cough. "Damn it," she said.

Sheila raised her face and whispered, "I'm going to get on him." She squatted over him and forced his penis into her vagina, beginning to move herself up and down on top of him.

Eleanor freed a hand from the camera and began to touch herself through her skirt, but when she realized what she was doing, she stopped.

Barbara, watching Sheila move against the man, dragged her fingernails across his chest, drawing blood. Sheila began to whine loudly but after a few moments quit moving and said, "Damn it." She looked down at him and said, "I'm afraid he's not going to. . . . Come on baby, for me, for me," and she began moving again, slightly faster this time.

Barbara sank off and to the side of his face and sat there fingering herself and slapping the bridge of his nose every few moments. When he came, Sheila smiled and pulled free of his penis. She straightened so that she could watch his semen slip out of her and onto his belly. "He came," she announced.

"I got it all," Eleanor said. "Every moment of it."

"Let's shove something up his ass," Barbara said.

"No. Let's untie him and go."

"Look at his face," Sheila said. "Peaceful." She ran her fingers through the semen and then smeared it against her vagina. Eleanor began to untie him, and after a moment, Sheila rose and gathered his clothes.

"Let's go," Shelia said.

"Wait," Barbara said. She kneeled over his face again and this time pissed. His closed eyes squeezed more deeply shut and he turned his head to the side.

"Why do you have to do that?" Sheila asked. "Why do you always have to do something like that?"

Barbara shrugged. "Don't ask why," she said. "Do you ask why about any of it?"

JOHN SCHOOL

The first time I was caught they told me I could go to john school so I wouldn't have all the legal hassle. The idea was that all us solicitors would sit around and listen to ex-prostitutes tell us about what a lousy life they had when they worked the streets and how unsafe it was for them and how it was unsafe for us. They had all kinds of stories about hating men, and one said she always kept a butcher knife under her bed and would fantasize about sticking it in the guy while he fucked her. She said that she had a friend who did the same thing and who finally did stab some guy in his ass.

"Where do you think that guy went?" she asked us, pushing her eyebrows up against her badly cut bangs. "Go to the hospital and say, oh, a whore just stabbed me? What's he going to tell his wife?"

She offered a dramatic pause.

"'Cause all you guys got rings on, don't you? What did you tell your wives you're doing today?"

I didn't have to come up with an excuse. I am not like those guys trying to get away from someone back home. I just like to get pussy that way. I like to get a woman to put her ass in the air and let me do what I like to it for fifty bucks. That was what separated me from the rest of the men in that room.

Anyway, they went around like that, talking about all the guys who they'd let fuck them without rubbers for twenty more bucks, and one of them even said she was dying of

AIDS. She didn't look like she was dying. I mean, they all looked like they were dying, but not from AIDS or anything like that. Anyway, I didn't pay much attention. I was hung over and bored. All these ex-whores gone fat with lousy hair-cuts and K-Mart suits made me feel bad all right, but not about fucking them for money. I felt worse about what they were doing now to pay their rents.

But then this one—Kay—who seemed the head of it all, was different. Whatever it was that makes it all go bad had-n't gotten to her yet. She didn't have a beat down look on her face and her makeup was done up all right and her skirt went just above her knees and she even showed a bit of cleavage. As she summed up what the other girls had said, she looked from face to face, and when she got to mine I didn't look away. I thought, Jesus, I'd like to fuck her. I knew it would-n't be as easy as slipping her fifty bucks or even a hundred, but there had to be a way. Knowing that it would be diffi-cult made the idea of it seem even more attractive.

The whole thing broke up and we all went our own ways, but I waited outside for her to come out.

"Kay?" I said.

She didn't want to see me. She didn't want to see anybody. It was twilight and she was standing there with all the tough worn off her, looking tired but still sexy.

"Yeah?"

"I'd like to hear more about it. What do you say, coffee?"

She sighed and shrugged. She was tired, like the rest of them.

"Come on," I said. "It's early. It would do me some good."

"All right."

We'd said coffee but we ended up in a bar right at the edge of downtown. It was ironic that two blocks away whores were walking up and down the street with their asses and tits bound up in tight balls of fabric. Long legs poking out. Slick inside, and easy.

But my mind was on Kay. She was still doing the gig, even though we were drinking. She said she was putting her life together, taking community college classes three days a week, working as the john school coordinator, renting an apartment closer to the water, taking care of a cat, hadn't done a drug in three years and only drank socially. But she was putting it away pretty well. I pretended to listen, but I was staring at her throat and her lips and thinking about the fact that she'd swallowed come for money. And I noticed that one of her buttons had opened so the curve of her tits was really showing.

I kept nodding my head and thinking about how much I wanted to duck my head beneath the table and look at her legs and maybe up her skirt. I wanted to see her panties, her cunt, her asshole.

She'd stopped talking and was stirring her drink. Her eyes had gone a little distant. She looked thirty-five, maybe a little older. She seemed to be growing edgy, as if a sudden sound would cause her to jump. I got to obsessing about seeing more of her flesh. Christ, I thought, if she'd only open another button, I would be happy.

We drank for a while and those thoughts grew in my mind. Sometimes she'd smile or something, but she spent more and more time staring kind of blankly at her drink as if she were avoiding a conversation that was forcing its way into her head.

Finally, it just came out. I said, "You got to be struggling a bit, with the classes and all, which I admire. I tell you what, I'd like to give you some money. I've got a good job. You seem like a nice lady and all." And I took twenty dollars out of my wallet and put it on the table between us.

"I can't take your money." There was the hint of some-thing defeated in her voice. The money was already in her purse, I knew, even if it sat there between us.

"Listen," I said, "if you don't feel good about taking it for nothing, then maybe you could do something for it. Something small. Maybe you could unbutton another button on your blouse, that's all. I mean, I know it goes contrary to what we've been talking about all day. But I just don't see it hurting either of us."

She didn't say anything. I thought maybe I'd made a mistake. I thought maybe my career in john school was over—Christ, for all I knew, she would call somebody and get me kicked out and then I'd have to go through a legal mess.

But then she picked up the money and put it in her purse and undid the button on her blouse. She looked into my eyes, I guess to see how it affected me. Her eyes had hardened a bit. I smiled and looked at her bra. It was black, and I felt like I knew everything I needed to know.

She kind of shook her head slowly, then took a drink. "Happy?"

"Yeah."

She was still trying to decide who had gotten the best of whom, I could see.

"Listen," I said, leaning forward, "I can give you more than that. If you take off your panties and give them to me, I'll give you fifty."

"Fuck you," she said.

I smiled. "Hey, you could use it, I could use it. Again, nobody gets hurt."

She took another drink. She frowned and let her eyes drop. She fingered the button she had undone on her blouse. She got up and walked away. Maybe she was leaving. Maybe she was going to the bathroom. I put fifty dollars on the table and finished my drink. Not knowing what to expect was exciting. When she came back, she put her fist toward me and I took her bunched up panties from it. Then I put them in my pocket. She took her fifty.

Now we both drank for a while. I glanced down at the opening in her shirt and thought about the fact that I was holding panties which had been pressed against her pussy. I was hard. I moved around so that my dick pressed against my leg or my forearm or the table. Jesus, I hadn't felt so good in a long time.

Her hair had gone a little limp. Her face glistened. Her lipstick was smeared from the corner of her mouth like a cut had opened there. We ordered more drinks. After I paid for them, I took out another fifty and put it on the table.

"Spread your legs, let me look," I said.

I didn't even pretend to drop anything. I just stuck my head under the table and stared at her knees. I figured she could pocket the money and do nothing if she wanted to, just keep those knees pressed together, white and round. My stomach was fluttering.

She opened her legs. Slowly—she knew what she was doing. She knew how to make me want more. Slowly. It was all shadow down there; I could see her inner thighs, but then nothing more.

I peeked up and whispered, "Hey, you have to lift your skirt a bit."

She did. There it was. The lips hung in a nest of black hair. Between them was that little black line and at its top, the flesh nugget of her clit. I could imagine getting my hands on it; in fact, it was everything I could do not to reach over and grab her, or thrust my face up close, where it wanted to be, and smell her. My dick was throbbing. I didn't care who heard or saw, I said, "I've got fifty more—lift your hips, thrust yourself forward, open it up."

And she did. The little black gap growing. She brought her hand down there and opened it up for me even more and slipped a finger inside. I felt like I might die, it was so good. I sat up. She went still, but I shook my head, "Go on," I said. "More."

I could see the shrugging motion in her shoulder as she began fingering herself. Her face was blank for a moment longer, but then, as if she knew just what I needed, she begin to bite her lip and slit her eyes.

"Good," I said, "good." I was rubbing myself like crazy now.

Then I came. A lot. Sticky, and almost immediately going cold. She stopped as soon as she saw I had. We sat there for a second. She took a drink.

Christ, everything had cracked, it always does. Her make-up, her smile, her eyes. Everything was gone.

I got up.

"Hey," she said. She wanted the other fifty, I imagined. I took it out. I left it on the table. "Wait," she said. And it occurred to me, as I walked away, that she wanted to earn that fifty—or to earn more. She wanted me to come with her to some place. Or worse, that she wanted to sit and talk like regular people in a regular place leading regular lives. I didn't care what she wanted. My dick was shriveling, my sense of self, my sense of her, of everything was shriveling.

I walked down the street thinking about what I'd done and kind of regretting it. It took another fifteen minutes for me to get horny again. She would be gone by now. It didn't matter, she was ruined, I didn't want her. Two blocks away, girls were walking up and down the street. They'd do anything I asked for just a little money.

But, hell, I wasn't that horny.

EVERY MOTHER'S SON

I'm twenty-five, but that doesn't mean I know myself. A great genius claimed to have remembered the womb and being born, but I don't remember anything like that. Maybe that's because I'm not a great genius, or a great anything, for that matter. I'm looking at a photo of my mother's cunt. It's heavy and soft looking, not of the sort I'd usually choose to dwell on. Still, she's in the proper pose. I like photos when the woman is on her knees with her torso sunk to the ground and her ass raised. It was only after I clicked on this picture to enlarge it that I recognized the table in my parents' study. Sitting on it are figurines of a little old man and a little old woman. Each is stopped slightly forward and shaped so that if you put them in the right positions, they seem to be sharing a kiss, his lips to her slightly red cheek.

I was sick as a kid and my parents tell me that many times I nearly died. Since the day I was born, I was in and out of the hospital, and I knew nothing of the life of a normal kid. There were problems with my lungs and a problem with my heart, other problems here and there. Nobody ever figured out where all this bad health came from. It was not in the family history—not in my mother or father, and not in what they knew of their parents, or the people who came before. What I didn't spend of those first ten years in the hospital, I spent in the house, and I can remember holding those figurines of the old man and woman and knowing enough about my condition to realize that I might never be old.

Then I turned ten, and within a year, my troubles had stabilized. Within another year, they were over. I was normal then and I've been normal since. It was the grace of God my mother has told me, but I don't know if she believes in God. My father, when he talks about those first ten years, gets tears in his eyes. They were young then themselves, eighteen when I was born, and when I look at pictures from that time in our lives, I can see in their faces what looks to me like both innocence and concern. I realize they spent most of their youth worrying about whether I would live or die, and it is hard to imagine anything else in their lives.

Now here I am looking at my mother's cunt. Her asshole is visible too. I realize that it is my father taking the picture, and I know enough about these kind of photos to understand that he is probably naked and has a hard-on. I've got one myself, though I had it before the picture came up, and I'm not certain I will keep it. My father has either just fucked my mother or he is about to fuck her. These are the people that made me, and this is how. Whatever I am was cooked up in there, some mix they made between them. Sometimes, when I don't feel good about who I am, I want to imagine that the bad things I see of myself are mine only, that they don't inhabit the people who came before me or the people I've chosen to be around me.

I close my eyes and think of my own wife and our six-month-old daughter. They sleep in the next room, which feels miles away on these occasions when I sit in the dark staring at the swingers' website. I've visited it from time to time since just after we got married. I can't imagine that my wife would ever agree to participate, but I masturbate to photos of other people's wives. I also masturbate to the idea of my wife being thus exposed, and to the idea of watching some other man with her. I don't know why I like these thoughts, but I do know that I can't show this side myself to my wife. She is of the world of light and that part of me is of the world of darkness, and it is, of course, best not to bring them together.

I think about the saying that all the great monsters of history were once some mother's baby. And of course even those of us who are not great monsters were some mother's baby, too.

I look at the photo of my mother taken by my father and think about that imperfect me they made and loved and worried over all through their youths. I think without wanting to of the birth of my own child, that mess of blood and mucus in which she was born and the way her head was elongated from the suction cup with which they pulled her out. At that moment, I thought that I'd put bad genes into a good girl and made something awful, but then the feeling melted, and I realized there was something purely good in front of me. I kissed my wife and the dirty baby that screamed as they vacuumed grit from the womb out of its mouth. Sometimes when I look at her now I get a strange feeling in my stomach over the idea that she is made of the same stuff I am and that I don't know exactly what that stuff is.

I look at the door and I know I could go through it. The room is cool. I could lie down beside them and my hard-on would go and I would re-join them in their innocence. It's tempting, though I don't know why anymore than I know why I feel the need to look back at the computer screen.

I press my fingers into my dick and my dick presses back and then I am stroking. It feels bad and good. I stare hard at the cunt and the asshole and sometimes it is my mother's and sometimes it belongs to any strange woman whose husband wanted to see her exposed and possessed by another man. Sometimes I see the future cunt of my wife from the angle of the man, me, who has convinced her to open it and let it be photographed and to put it up for other people to see in hopes that one of them will agree to come and fuck it. Sometimes I only see flesh. But when I come, it is to my mother's cunt. I have the feeling, just for a moment, of everything in the world being truly in order; the feeling that some terrible but obvious secret has been whispered to me and that holding it in my ear has made me powerful. But then the secret feels false and I lose it. I began to realize that I don't know anything, not even what these, my own desires, really mean.

I come for a long time, perhaps four or five seconds.

When I finish, I hear myself say "Mom." It's more of a cry. Now I feel a sadness. I put my dick back in my pants. I stand and turn on the lights and feel I must bathe in them before I can go into the room with my wife and child. What comes to me is a memory. It is of the Fourth of July of the first year after I was fully better and my mom and my dad were in high spirits. We went to the mountains and built a fire and cooked marshmallows and shot off little fountains and lit sparklers and then we sat together under the stars singing songs. It seemed at that time that all the big questions of the world had been answered. There was a point when I thought to myself, if this was a story of my life, of all of our lives, this would be a good place for it to end.

NO ANGEL

Baby cried nearly all the time, but it was his silence that woke her from a nap in the afternoon. She rose and looked into his crib and saw a grasshopper kick as if to leap up and out the cabin window through which it must have come. It appeared caught in some pinch, and she realized its lower thorax had been crushed against the yellow blanket. It tried to leap again and failed and tried again. Baby lay on his side, still strangely tranquil, his eyes staring from huge and sunken sockets half hidden behind thin, yellow eyelids. Baby's long fingers—sharp looking—curled and uncurled beside the grasshopper. It raised a single front leg which shuddered pointing skyward. The kind thing to do would be to squeeze its head, but the thought of it made her dizzy.

For a moment she could not recognize Baby as her own, nor could she recognize the cabin or anything in this place, and she felt, as she sometimes did, utterly lost.

Now it is near dusk and Daddy comes through the door. Where he got the name Daddy she doesn't know, and she can't imagine what name came before that, but there must have been one, for, as far as she believes, every human coming into this world is given a Christian name. Even Baby has one; it doesn't matter if they use it or not. Daddy does not look at her but back through the open doorway, as if he believes some forest thing has shadowed him home.

Daddy has always been just as he is now. She remembers nothing different about him, even from the times when she was a little girl herself and the daddy they shared still lived. The old man was sick for most of those years, propped up in the bed in the corner of the cabin, creaking out his complaints at her and Daddy: *I'm hungry. What you bring for me to eat? Nothing at all? She starving me to death on cornbread and the like that just fall into my belly and crumple up in there and come right out through me as the mush it was. Her momma—God rest—fed me for proper. I got now ghost blood in my veins and not the strength to lift my arm and change my own pillow. And you. You go out there come back and bring me nothing but the smell of the woods? Can't you find you any beast? Can't kill any meat at all, even a rabbit or a squirrel?*

Daddy turns and stands for a little while in the door without looking at her, as if he also hears the rattle of the old man's voice in his head. Daddy looks much like what the old man must have looked like when he was that age, except that Daddy has always looked just as old as he is now and will never look older. He was maybe fourteen when she began to remember him, but his face and limbs were hard and creased and red even then, as if he had been strapped to a rock in the sun as a child and baked there.

He brings with him the smell of the woods, the smell which has hung over this place, the only place she's known, all her life.

Daddy lays the rabbit skins down on the table. The backs of them are run through with lines of blood like a net of veins peeled from the muscle and fingernail-sized slabs of white and almost yellow fat. He studies them like some map of the journey on which he's been, or some primal painting of the hunt itself. Then he turns to her with sharp eyes.

She wonders if he already knows what she found during her pee this morning.

Daddy says, "He's quiet. Usually I hear him screaming out from down the path like he's calling me home."

He unslings the skinned rabbit bodies from his shoulder and puts them on the windowsill, where the wood is dark. Then he turns to the cradle. He leans down and reaches in with one hand to touch Baby. As he does, she gets the impression he is hiding something in his other hand.

"You blocking the sun from Baby."

He stands and looks at her defiantly, but then drops his eyes and moves away from Baby and the window. "There ain't much left. Why he so quiet?"

"Maybe he's screamed himself out. More likely, he'll be back at it again tomorrow or sooner."

Daddy nods.

The rabbits, slick and seared in the sunlight, are, like the back of their skins, run through with webs of red and chunks of white and even, she notices, patches of blue. She imagines putting them back together, matching gore to gore. Though she knows what she sees now is muscle and that muscle is meat and that meat, food, the bodies of these rabbits do not look like anything she can eat, or even name, but something unworldly, some mistake of heaven abandoned in shame to this world.

"I wish you wouldn't always bring them in here. They scare Baby. Skins too—you just going to tack them up outside in the morning. Why we got to smell them in here all through the night?"

"Smell of life. And ain't nothing like that scares Baby. He ain't been spoilt toward that yet. They just things to him. If I were to put one of them rabbits down in that blanket with him, he would look at it and touch it and put his mouth against it and try to know it." He gives her another defiant look, but then turns away and puts something in his pocket. She knows it is a rabbit's foot. He mumbles, "Ain't been spoilt toward this world."

He walks over by the stove and rubs his hands above it though he can't see that no fire burns there.

"How you feel today?"

"I feel better today."

"It's been how long since you had that loss?"

"I don't know. Two months, maybe. I got my first blood since then this morning."

His eyes slit as he considers the blood, and she sees the hunger in him surface. He nods his head and turns back to Baby and the rabbits in the window and the falling sun.

She dreams sometimes of the second baby—lost now two months to the day—and it is always fat and bronze with eyes of deep green and golden locks and a serious mouth; the edges of wings poke through the skin of its shoulder blades. She delivered not this imagined child but an ugly, twisted being, as if some jealous or angry or simply stupid thing had gotten in there and tortured it while it was supposed to form into the one perfect thing. Daddy buried it not in back of the cabin by their parents' graves, but somewhere in the woods—she didn't now where, though she knew someday she would. He'd given it no words because it was not human and had never been, and said she should not worry because when she was well again they would make another which would be right and ready like Baby.

Though Baby ain't right, she thought then and thinks sometimes now.

"You ain't going to give him that rabbit paw."

He puts both hands in his pockets and shrugs. "No, I weren't thinking that. You can have it if you want it."

"I don't want it. They say it bring luck, but that don't mean nothing to me. Luck and blessing is two different things and what we need is blessing."

She walks over to Baby and sees a red print on the child's pale and sunken chest, like a tear opening from the nipple. "You left blood on Baby."

"Well, he come into the world in blood. He probably leave the world in blood. He ain't no angel, is he?"

"What you mean, no angel?" She thinks again of what she had imagined the second baby would be like. Its perfection explodes into a vision of blinding gold. She stumbles a sightless step forward before she can see the cabin and Daddy again.

He looks at her for a while and turns back to the cold stove. She knows he's given her room since the miscarriage and the sickness that followed; she also knows that the type of tenderness he's offered her since then cannot last as long as she'd like it to.

"Ain't nobody here an angel," he says quietly. "I learned that. What you think angels eat? How you think they live? Not like us. We ain't that privileged. Just a man. A boy. A baby before that. And so Baby will be a boy and then a man like me. And when he is a man like me he will make from himself more like him and like me and you too. And ain't none of them that won't be born in blood and live in blood. And die in blood."

"You hush up, why don't you, and get us a fire started."

"I come tired, wandering since morning the clay flats for those two rabbits. You going to cook them if I do light the stove?"

Again, she is caught in the dizziness. She feels almost relieved, as if in this whirling she will be lifted from this life into something better, cleaner, some place without blood. . . .

She steadies herself against the cradle.

Baby's mouth opens in a scowl of a yawn, and a gurgle comes out twisting into a belch, spewing a white liquid that runs down the side of his face. He closes his mouth and eyes, and he rolls his head to one side. The white liquid is thin and phosphorous of smell. She can see that in there are chunks of something in it, though she can't think of what. She can't remember feeding him anything. She realizes at this moment she cannot think of feeding him anything ever. She cannot think of what his name is beside Baby; and then she cannot remember even that; she cannot remember how he was born or conceived. She cannot think of anything at all except that the cabin smells of raw flesh. And the sun is gone.

EXPLOITER

My old man lived off the animals. He used to run a trap line and raise chinchillas in the basement. He shot bears for the gallbladders, deer and elk for their horns, and God knows what else. Cockfights, dog fights, raccoons chained to logs forced to fight dogs, and so on. He ran exotic birds through the house; they'd come by the hundreds, though only a dozen or so would still be alive, and my father and I would burn the dead bodies and try to clean up those who had lived. Then somebody would pick them up and give my father money. Mother kept a few, her pets, and taught them to speak, so that they were different.

She got fed up after a while, probably with all the animals and the death and the fact that my father never had a real job and most of the money we had as a family wasn't legitimately earned. I think she wanted to lead a regular life. And so she left.

I was seventeen. The morning after she went, my father moved from bird to bird, wringing their necks. I guess he didn't want them bringing up memories.

Those first seventeen years were steeped in blood and suffering and death. It could have been my birthright. You'd think I'd be the same as my old man. But I wasn't. Those pet birds who could talk, the sound of their necks breaking, was the end of it.

And so, like my mother, I left.

Ten years later and I don't eat meat or wear leather. Or wool, for that matter, or silk. I don't eat eggs, don't drink milk. I try not to do anything which has ties to the exploitation of animals. I like to believe I'm not reacting against anything but an overall state of unfairness in the world. I like to believe that even if I had grown up the regular way my mother wanted these convictions would have grown in me.

I am involved. I am doing what I can. I have stolen and destroyed things. I have broken as a thief and vandal into testing laboratories, hen batteries, fur farms. Trying to slip cogs out of the machine, trying to remember that each individual suffering is worth alleviating, even if the overall problem is not solved. Sometimes we go beyond those actions. Sometimes we do things that would make lesser people turn away. But I am certain. Nothing will make me stop.

It is only that I need a break. Everybody has his vacation.

Ten years and I haven't seen my old man who moved into a cabin we owned in a Washington state forest. I call him two or three times a year. We never really talk about anything. The calls are just to confirm that he is alive. It's obvious he's gone downhill. You can hear the age in his voice. I imagine empty cages with doors bent open, instruments that were once sharp and shiny now dull and rusted. It is important for me to believe that my father has not been able to continue his career as an exploiter. He'd be a perfect target, but I love him—that can't be helped.

The cabin is in a state of disrepair, and to my relief there are no apparent victims around—nothing staked to the ground, nothing stretched on the outside walls, nothing crying out from some hidden place—nothing. Instead, butterflies and hummingbirds and fat flies dart through the air.

He's bent, the old man, and all gray. Hair hangs off his knuckles and out of his ears. His face is mean and wrinkled and when he smiles at me from the cabin door it looks like a rubber mask. Something that might scare you at first but that a moment later you might find completely devoid of threat.

What you up to, Pop?

I've got to tell you, he says in the voice of a conspirator. A fear runs through me—that I've found particular signs. Absolute evidence. He is about . . .

Who's about?

He hisses it: Bigfoot.

The relief is not as heavy as you might think. In truth, I am surprisingly undone by the pathos of it. My old man sitting there, his eyes twinkling and mouth curling in a grin. The old man all broken down and questing after some mythical beast. For a moment, I try to imagine that Bigfoot is indeed about. Worse, I hope that my father will catch him. That the light—mean and stupid as it is—will not leave his eyes.

Going to get him by God!

The old man's face is so steady and certain now that I can't find the pathos any longer, and I'm chilled by his certainty and intensity.

He feeds me potatoes and I ignore the bloody, store-bought meat he eats. Afterwards, he shows me cutouts from various tabloids offering various sums of money for the live capture, or at least the dead body, of Bigfoot.

Artists' renderings show him sad-eyed and intelligent-looking. His face reminds me of the many chimps I've seen tortured and imprisoned. His shoulders are slumped, as if he is perpetually tired of hiding from those that search. At night, his sad face comes to me, as it is in the drawings, but then transforms, and I can see the cruelty of my father's eyes and the stupidity of his hungry grin.

My old man sits by the window, staring out. Slack has drawn the wrinkles from his face and his eyes appear deep and thoughtful. His lips are puckered, his head cocked slightly. I can see a slight tremble in his earlobe.

Each morning, my father goes across an old bridge and into the forest. He carries a carefully maintained tranquilizer gun—I've used them myself in vastly different circumstances—and a backpack. He's hunched and hunkered and disappears into the woods.

At night, I hear noises from the forest; they wake me from my sleep and I think about the creature. My father is always awake at these times and staring out the window.

When I dream at night, it is of my old man or Bigfoot. It is often a combination of the two, the face alternately evil and innocent, mean and sad. I also dream of animals, mostly those I could not reach or that were found to be so far gone the only thing to do for them was to kill them. It wears me out so that when I wake I feel I haven't slept at all. I wait for my father during the day. Frequently, I drift into naps, and I dream then too. I dream not only of animals, but of humans, the ones I've tried to break in body and in mind.

Sometimes I wake still dreaming. I think of all the pain to which I've been witness.

Then I snap from it to the sound of birds, to the smell of my father, and, sometimes, to a deeper smell, as if some more musty creature is in the forest. I feel watched, frightened, bare.

The old man comes back limping. He doesn't know to soak his feet. Going to get him, he says, you bet. He eats his bloody meat. He stares from the window.

At night, something thrashes a challenge in the woods. A week ago, I would have known it was only a deer or an elk. Now I am not so certain.

I am not sleeping enough. Those dreams follow me too far into waking. The sunlight is on my face but I can look right past it to the woods, where moss hangs like drapes and darkness abounds, where the stink of earth is blinding. I've been weak before, many times. During almost any campaign, there is a moment of weakness. But weakness is something a good mind can overcome.

Overcome, I tell myself. Think straight. Take control. Overcome.

I decide to do something. I love my old man, but I hate what he stands for. When I wait for an hour and then track him into the forest, I don't know if I go with love for him or with hate for what he has done and what he plans to do. I don't know if I go to kill the sad beast in him or the mean beast in him. I don't even know if I go believing that I am not only a follower, but the followed, as if the creature my old man pursues might in fact be pursuing me, using my father as simple bait.

My mind is not clear on any of that.

I know only that we will meet in the forest and I will break the old man's neck.

I've done it before, to both man and animal, to put an end to some kind of misery. I cross the bridge with that one thing in mind.

There was a light rain last night and into this morning, and his recent tracks are easy to differentiate.

This forest is dark and crowded and dank. There is the drone of insects and the sound of small animals, and sometimes, there is the sound of something much larger moving out of sight. Mind clear, I tell myself, body go forward. One step after the other.

I see a thin stand of aspen trees with sunshine pouring in. My father's tracks veer off there, and I follow them. He is fifty yards in, lying at the base of a tree, his hands folded on his chest, his pack and rifle propped up beside him. Up close, I can hear his breath, long and deep. I look around. The woods are still. My father is still. I think I can hear his heart. Or perhaps it is my own. Or perhaps it is the heartbeat of the creature. For a moment, I imagine that I am the bigfoot my old man seeks. I imagine standing above my father, leaning down with large, black hands and twisting, without much might, the old man's head so that his neck snaps and it is over.

And I hear all of our hearts as that one heart.

A small black ant runs across my old man's face, and I realize he's going to die, just like that, without really causing much more harm to the world. I realize that if the creature watches in the dark of the forest, it is safe and knows it.

Okay, I say. All right.

And walk away.

HUNGER

He had once shared with a friend his penchant for anal sex, and was immediately labeled an "ass-fucker." He hated the term. It was a compulsion he did not try to explain. He always practiced it in the dark and always followed it up with a shower in the dark as well. He recognized in it a certain irony: the act of eating, not to mention shitting, repulsed him. For this reason, he was very thin, living almost completely off of protein shakes and salads. His wife, on the other hand, had grown very fat. They hadn't had sex of any kind for over a year.

She blamed her eating on a series of miscarriages and the doctor's prognosis that they would never have children. She had been slightly plump when they met, but by now she had grown huge. He had masturbated to cable porn for so long it no longer had the power to inspire him sexually, and in a desperate bid to reconnect in a sexual way with his wife, he decided to touch her again. She was sleeping on her side. He pushed against the mass of her until she was mostly on her stomach, and then he lifted her nightshirt. Her calves were as big as his thighs, and her thighs were as big as his waist. His lust was mightier than his distaste. He could think of nothing but the idea of sinking into that dirty place inside of her. The skin of her ass was slack and dimpled and he discovered that, push it aside as he might, he could not locate her asshole. He quickly went limp as he stared down at her.

Something had to be done.

He made arrangements for two weeks of sick and vacation leave from work, and asked a friend to meet him with spare car keys at a place they camped once a year. He packed the trunk of the car in secret. Then he drove his wife into the mountains under the guise of a trip to pick berries and mushrooms. She was a meat eater—had gorged on bacon and sausage and leftover steak for breakfast—and the trip did not appeal much to her. She complained of hunger the entire way. It caused him alternating waves of sorrow and anger. When they arrived at the camping spot, he parked the car, then got out and dropped the keys in the gas tank.

It stunned even him for a moment.

"Now," he said, "we're going to do this together. We're going to stay out here fourteen days and live off mushrooms and berries, and we're going to break you of this addiction you have to great quantities of fattening food." He'd said it just as he had rehearsed it, and as he watched her mouth—a small cut in the hills of flesh that were her cheeks—fall open, he added, impromptu, "This is an intervention of sorts."

In the tent, her sobs kept him awake half that night. He had developed a dependence on sleeping pills. When he examined this addiction, he told himself it was because of the noises her body made, the gurgling of her stomach and the other movement of gasses through her, but he knew that in all honesty his trouble with sleeping went deeper than that. In any case, he'd brought plenty of pills to get him through the fourteen nights. He took two now and was sound asleep before he had to endure her wailing and the shaking of her massive body for long.

She was listless throughout the following day, and he had to remind himself why he was doing this. It was for the future; they would suffer now and reap the rewards later.

"You don't understand my kind of hunger," she told him.

"You don't understand that I want more than to sleep beside you. I want to want you. I want to do what I used to do, which is get a hard-on thinking of you."

She turned her head away, perhaps from the word "hard-on." He moved in closer to her. "I want to look at you and think about how badly I want to fuck you. Yes, fuck you!"

"I'm starving!" she screamed, and then burst into tears.

"Please. It's okay. This will make us better. I'm going to take you to the Virgin Islands. You'll get into bathing suits you haven't gotten into for years. We'll lie on the beach in the sunlight and everything will be beautiful. From when we leave here onward, we'll live differently." He could imagine it. They would start their morning with grapefruit. The refrigerator would be filled with bottled water and fruits and vegetables; there would be grapes, kiwi, strawberries; there would be lettuce and tomatoes and carrots. He got more than a bit hungry thinking about these things. He thought instead about how her ass had once been and how it would be again, and the thought of fucking it was as exciting to him as the thought of fucking it the first time had been.

He took her thick hand in his. "Two weeks is a short price to pay for changes that will last a lifetime."

"What about the fish?" she asked.

"What?"

"Our fish."

"Oh. I didn't remember to think about them. I guess they'll be little skeletons when we get back. We'll get more. Here now, eat these berries. They're delicious."

The second night was much the same as the first, only now she was whimpering instead of wailing. He took an extra half-dose of his pills, and still it seemed he could not sleep. An old frustration crept into him and he glanced at her angrily, but then his mind began to cloud and he knew if he'd let everything go for just a moment, he would sleep. It was overly warm in the tent, and there was a strange odor. He told himself that none of it mattered; he told himself to sleep. In the end, he took out another pill, and with this he finally drifted away, though having used so many pills caused a sickly feeling in him.

In the afternoon of the following day, she sat hunched over, her face very pale, her teeth clutching her bottom lip to control her crying. He thought he could see a bit of thinness in her cheeks, and he smiled. He collected mushrooms and surprised her with cubed bullion that he'd secretly brought and now put in a pan of water on the fire.

That night, her stomach howled in such monstrous tones that it brought him fully awake. He heard an animal scurry in the forest as if it too had been frightened by her belly. He'd never get back to sleep now, even if he took another pill.

That day she was even more morose. She did not cry but sat crossed legged, rocking back and forth, and would not speak to him except for a few words. Sometimes her eyes rolled up to the sky and around it as if she was searching for something.

"You're not going to frighten me," he said. "I'm okay, so I know you are."

Her eyes fixated on him, but they jiggled in such a way that they actually did frighten him. He did not want to show his concern and so looked away. "This hunger," she said. "You have no way of knowing."

Even he did not find the berries and mushrooms filling. "It's all in the mind," he said as they ate a batch for lunch. "Food should be merely nutrition. There are more important things in life." She stared at the cut of mushroom withering up in the pan on the fire.

"Like what?"

"Well," he said. "Love. Sex."

"Is that all?"

"Let's see. No. There is the pleasure of sleep."

"Love," she murmured. "Sex. Sleeping."

They went on for several more days. She continued with the relative silence and often fell to staring at the sky. Sometimes she wandered off into the woods, and he assumed it was to piss and shit and did not follow her. His own feces had turned to mush, which bothered him. He could imagine the beauty of a life without the need to shit at all. He smiled thinly, thinking about it.

She was sitting on a log and staring into her lap, whispering something. That she might, after several more days like this, try to hunt down and kill something occurred to him, but he doubted that she would be successful.

He studied her for thinness, and thought he could see places where there was less of her. Her belly, her breasts, her upper arms. To be sure, the skin was slack there, but that slackness would go eventually. She would someday again be the woman he married. He smiled to himself and drifted into a daydream in which she was lying face down on the bed, her ass raised on a pillow, turning her head to look back on him, and saying, "Thank you for what you did for us. Now fuck my ass."

That night, he slept uneasily. He had taken an entire extra dose of pills, but he kept half-waking to the impression that she was awake studying him. Her eyes were sunken the next morning—her entire face seemed sunken. Despite the fatigue and hunger (though he would not call it hunger) haunting him, he felt inspired.

"You look nice," he told her. "We're making progress."

She nodded her head. Her stomach screamed. He stepped away.

That evening, she grew tender with him. They sat by the fire and she pressed against him. She'd followed him around quietly all afternoon, and he assumed that she had been broken. "Honey," she whispered, over and over. Her voice was lulling. He drank the bullion and berry mash she'd made for him. He felt a sweet sense of sleepiness, the kind he did not want to let pass. He dug in the tent for his pills. The baggie was nearly empty. He took one, and then two, to be sure, and sat down beside her again. She was looking at him with what appeared to be love in her eyes. He had grown quite sleepy and found her eyes penetrating. There was something like love in them, and if his head wasn't so light, he would have been compelled to lean toward her and kiss her softly.

"I don't feel well," he heard himself saying, and he didn't. A nausea had come down on him.

"Lie down," she said. "You'll feel better."

She was still staring at him. She smiled. He recognized that it wasn't quite love she was showing him, but a kind of hunger. It was vaguely disconcerting, but he believed, as she bent toward him, that she would take care of him.

He woke without wanting to. The world was dark and yet he could feel that one side of him was overly warm. His eyes fell closed without having really taken anything in. He felt he needed to will them open and struggled to do so. Above him were spots of light—stars—and he wondered how he'd gotten out of the tent. He lolled his head to the side and saw a brighter light and realized that he looked at the fire, which was burning hotly. His eyelids began to fall. He meant to bring a hand up and rub it through them, but his hand would not move. Nor would his legs.

"What an odd dream," he thought. But he felt it was not a dream and he ought to look again. He blinked hard and then popped open his eyelids. Indeed, there were stars above. Indeed, the fire was to the side. Something was wrong. His stomach burned with hunger and his head was very light. He wanted to call out for her. He felt he needed her to hold his head and tell him it was all right. He began to drift back into unconsciousness when a scraping along his leg startled him.

He blinked and looked and saw his wife kneeling there. She'd pulled his pant leg up and was washing the area below his knee. He tried to excuse it all as dream, but he knew it was not. There was something terrible in her face, an exaggeration of the look of hunger she'd given him earlier that night. She'd gone mad in some way. He decided he best rise and get away from her, but when he tried, he found he could not. He could not even kick his leg away from her touch. She looked at him, the hunger momentarily replaced by what he recognized as sorrow.

"What has happened?" he tried to ask.

"I'm sorry," she said. "I tried to give you enough so you'd sleep through it all."

"What?"

She looked at his leg again. The sadness fell away and the hunger was there. She dropped the cloth with which she'd been wiping at him and lifted a knife. "I told you that you can't understand this kind of hunger. I'll try not to take much. But there's just so little of you. Still, maybe it will be enough to get me through these final days. And I won't let you bleed. I'll use the fire."

He could hear the stream and he could hear the fire, and above him the stars came into sharp focus. Her stomach howled. The stars blurred and he began drifting toward grayness as he felt a tugging sensation at his calf.

WORMS

It doesn't matter who you are now. You sold them to fisher-
man for a penny apiece as a child. You dug them, faceless,
out of pitch-forked clods of dirt, from the time you were
seven until you were fifteen. At first, you used the money to
buy sodas and comic books; later you began to save the
majority of it for a time when you were old enough to retire
from worms and think about different kinds of work. You
used that money as part of the payment on your first car—
six hundred dollars. Sixty thousand worms.

What you do now doesn't matter. Six-hundred-thousand
worms that you can keep dollar track of, but probably
another five- or six-hundred-thousand more before that. You
learned in biology, when you had to dissect worms, that they
are built internally much in the same way you are. You saw
the small stomach, the heart, even the brain. You learned
that they have a central nervous system much like your own.
Nerves, pain receptors, all of it. Where were their faces,
where were their mouths? Through what could they cry
when they were impaled onto hooks? You remember they
often shit against the pain, although you did not then con-
sider it pain.

Now you've reached a level of consciousness that does not
allow you to think of a cow as meat and leather, or a fish as
a fillet, or a chicken as an egg-laying machine, or even a
horse as something meant merely to carry you from one
place to another. You've tried to add in your head all the farm

animals for whose deaths you are responsible—fifteen or twenty full cows; two dozen or so pigs; probably three geese and five turkeys; a duck; approximately fifty chickens . . . all these deaths you attribute to yourself can't possibly reach over two hundred, which is overwhelming in its own way.

Still, the worms haunt you the most. You know now they suffer pain the same way a cow—or a pet dog for that matter—can suffer pain, and you wonder how you will ever make up for the million or so you sacrificed to soda pops and your first car; how can you forgive yourself for the agony of your youth for which you still, despite everything, sometimes feel nostalgic?

You go out walking in the rain, picking them up from the sidewalk where they go to escape drowning; you pick them up, a few hundred from the hundreds of thousands littering the asphalt and the cement of the city, and you put them where you hope they will be safe, on the grass, on the dirt beneath the branches of a tree.

Even on a sunny day when the worms are invisible, you put your hand to the warm grass and you sense that the ground is full of them. The earth, covered with living things, is itself alive, moving, and strong, and sufficient. In it you sense most keenly, as you do in all life, the potential for suffering. You can feel the pain through your fingers.

You walk in the rain lifting worms.

THE END

J. Eric Miller grew up in a cabin in the mountains of Colorado, son of a miner and a taxidermist. He holds a Ph.D. in English from the University of Denver. After teaching literature and creative writing for two years at the American University of Beirut, J. Eric Miller is now an assistant professor of screenwriting at Kennesaw State University. His short fiction has appeared in a wide variety of literary magazines and ezines. *Animal Rights and Pornography* is his first book.

Printed in the United States
By Bookmasters